Tao had not really thought past getting Monique home safely. Sure, he had immediately noticed how hot she looked that night, with her bare back exposed and the thrust of her uncovered breasts teasing the fabric of her top. He had even had the chance to admire the sexy length of her legs in her very high heels. But, it had only been a natural appreciation of a beautiful woman. Not once had he really thought about holding her or kissing her. But now, standing just inside her house while she looked up at him with eyes more open and honest than ever before, her lips slightly parted, it was all he could think about.

Tao didn't hesitate to pull her close with a gentle hand behind her head. He placed his mouth on hers. It started out as a simple kiss, meant to test her interest in something more. But the second he brushed his lips across hers, it felt like pure electricity. Tao pulled back in surprise, hovering only an inch from her, trying to understand the jolt that hit him somewhere below his navel. Then, he kissed her again with no questions or hesitation.

Also by Sophia Shaw

MOMENT OF TRUTH

A RARE GROOVE

SHADES AND SHADOWS

DEPTHS OF DESIRE

Published by Kensington Publishing Corp.

WHAT LIES BETWEEN LOVERS

SOPHIA SHAW

Kensington Publishing Corp.

http://www.kensingtonbooks.com

DAFINA BOOKS are published by

Kensington Publishing Corp.
119 West 40th Street
New York, NY 10018

All Kensington Titles, Imprints, and Distributed Lines
are available at special quantity discounts for bulk purchases
for sales promotions, premiums, fund-raising, and educa-
tional or institutional use. Special book excerpts or cus-
tomized printings can also be created to fit specific needs.
For details, write or phone the office of the Kensington special sales manager: Kensington Publishing Corp., 119 West
40th Street, New York, NY 10018, attn: Special Sales
Department, Phone: 1-800-221-2647.

Dafina and the Dafina logo Reg. U.S. Pat. & TM Off.

ISBN-13: 978-0-7582-3476-6
ISBN-10: 0-7582-3476-7

First mass market printing: July 2009

10 9 8 7 6 5 4 3 2 1

Printed in the United States of America

In memory of my father,
Arnold Jackson
August 29, 1941 to March 1, 2008

ACKNOWLEDGMENTS

It's been a crazy year! I want to take a moment to thank all of my special friends and family who made it possible for me to survive it and be stronger in the end.

To my sisters, Gloria, Deon and Natasha—you were always there to listen patiently and give me the advice I needed. I couldn't have chosen better sisters and best friends.

To my brothers, Roland and Wayne—I can't thank you both for everything you have done for me and the girls. I can't think of a way to repay you, but I'm working on it!

To my friends, Rossana and Beverley—you knew exactly when I needed a good laugh or the hard, painful truth. We've been through so many ups and downs together over the years and I know I can survive anything because you both have my back.

To Trung—you asked for an Asian lover, and here he is! Thanks for sowing the seed.

To my mom, Dr. Iris Thomas—thank you for worrying about me, praying for me and the girls, and sharing your good advice. You are my inspiration and I love you.

To my agent, Sha-Shana Crichton—I want to thank you for your work and guidance over the years. You have been instrumental in making my dream come true.

To Keith—thank you for raising the bar. You inspired so many parts of this story, and I hope I have motivated you to finish yours.

To all the other important and influential people in my life, including my readers and supporters—I can't possibly mention all of you here, but I appreciate everything you contribute to my life and success.

Sincere regards,

Sophia

Inspire

I remain—
Uninspired by pavement
Glass and steel

Show me the sun
Reflected in the waves
Sparkling across the snow
Shining in my daughter's eyes

I remain—
Uninspired by conflicts
Debates and politics

Show me the deer
Dancing across the meadow
Chasing white tails
And butterflies

I remain—
Inspired by love
A woman's touch
And sometimes—
by pain

Keith Shier

Chapter 1

Did you ever end up in a bad situation, and have no clue how you got there? Did you spend hours wondering how things went so wrong, and why you did not see it coming until it was too late? Monique Evans had been asking herself the same questions for weeks now, and was still waiting for the answers.

She was fully engrossed in a few stolen moments of brooding when she heard her name mentioned somewhere off in the distance. It dragged her attention back to the penthouse-level conference room and to the dozen or so faces staring at her, waiting for her response to a question that she had not heard within a discussion she had not been listening to.

Monique blinked a few times, and then put a thoughtful look on her face. A little flutter of panic rose in her throat as several seconds ticked by and no appropriate answers came to mind. With the calculated practice of a seasoned salesperson, she searched for clues within the white boards and open presentations about what her clients wanted to hear. The silence stretched to the point where the coworker sitting beside her started to fidget in his seat.

"I want to make sure I understand your question before I go into detail," Monique finally stated while glancing at the most vocal participants in the meeting. "Can you put it into context for me?"

She was relieved when Robert Tomlin, the head of asset management for the Broadline Logistics, nodded with understanding.

"We would like the new system to have some open source code so that our own developers can customize the software as needed. Then, we need to understand how those customizations will affect your product guarantee."

Everything clicked for Monique at that moment. As the Director of Sales at Sector Asset Solutions, she was responsible for making sure their top clients, like Broadline, were happy with their software. This meeting was to close them on a full system upgrade, a project worth up to ten million dollars. Before her mind had wandered off to reflect on the current chaos of her personal life, Jeff Culvert, her Senior Systems Engineer, had been outlining the various upgraded features in the new version of SPIDER, Sector Asset's core product. Easy and flexible customization was one of the biggest selling features.

"Robert, as you know, our client satisfaction guarantee is the best in the business, and one of our key differentiators," she replied. "SPIDER Release 4 has been designed with that in mind. Because we can't control your customizations, we can only guarantee the functionality of our original code. But, as Jeff explained, the knowledge and document management modules of Release 4 make tracking all modifications very simple. As long as your developers meet the process requirements, we will be able to track any problems."

Without prompting, Jeff took over to delve deeper into the technical details of the issue. Monique listened intently, determined to stay focused, but prayed with every breath that the meeting would end soon. How many more questions could they still have after three solid hours of tech talk?

Her wish came true about ten minutes later. She and Jeff hung around after to chitchat for as long was appropriate, then they grabbed a cab to go back to Sector Asset. Jeff spent the short ride from San Diego's downtown core out to their office in Mission Hills checking messages on his Blackberry. Monique had her head turned toward the window, and she wore large, dark sunglasses to cover up her blank stare off into space.

This melancholy had been with Monique all day and really took her by surprise. It had been several weeks since she had finally felt over *him*. *Him* being Donald Sanderson, the boyfriend she had broken up with after almost three years together. It had been really hard at first, but Monique was finally feeling as though the whole messy affair was behind her.

Until today, anyway.

In her calendar, she had bookmarked the coming Saturday as her ideal wedding day. The reminder notice had popped up when she logged onto her computer that morning. It was a note made impulsively almost nine months earlier, after Donald had assured her they would be married before Thanksgiving. At the time, fully in love and looking for assurances, she had believed him. Several weeks later, Monique had finally accepted that all his promises were lies and he was never going to leave his wife.

"Are you going upstairs?" Jeff asked once they had exited the cab. "It's almost five-thirty."

He was fairly young, probably a couple of years younger than Monique's twenty-eight years, but one of the smartest engineers she had ever worked with. Unlike the other presales technicians in the company, Jeff knew how to explain complicated technology to the most clueless layperson.

"Yeah, I know," she replied. "But, I still have to review some reports for tomorrow morning."

"Well, don't work too late," Jeff advised before he jogged off to the parking lot with youthful energy.

Monique made her way to her office at a much slower pace. It was true that she had a little work to do, but she also had some time to burn before she had to be at her ball game later that evening. On Wednesdays, she played basketball in a recreational league, and tonight the game was scheduled to start at seven o'clock. That gave Monique enough time to wrap up a small project and get to the gym in time to change.

Her league played at the gymnasium at Balboa

Park in downtown San Diego. Monique arrived later than she had expected and rushed to change out of her business suit and into gym shorts, a sports bra, and her team jersey. The last thing she needed was to arrive on the court late and after the starting whistle. She was the only woman playing in an all-men's club, and she'd endured enough aggravation from the guys already.

When she was finally dressed, Monique hung up her work clothes in a locker, laced up her ball shoes, and sprinted out of the changing room. In her distracted haste, she almost ran into her friend and teammate, Gary Cooper, as he stepped out of the men's changing room next door.

"Whoa," he exclaimed, stepping back quickly to avert a collision.

"Hey, Coop," Monique stated, once she realized who it was. She slowed down to walk beside him.

"Everything all right?" Gary asked, looking her up and down.

"Yeah," she replied quickly. "Why?"

"Nothing," he told her. "You just look all made up, that's all. Are you trying to impress someone?"

Monique stopped dead in her tracks and quickly touched her cheeks in surprise.

"Oh, no," she moaned.

She had forgotten to wash the makeup off her face, which meant that her eyes were still lightly rimmed with dark liner and fringed with lashes thickened with mascara. Her lips were probably stained with deep brick-red gloss. Monique immediately rubbed off as much lip color as possible on the back of her hand, then looked back down the hall, clearly contemplating dashing back into the changing rooms.

"Don't worry about it. It's barely noticeable," Gary assured her. "Come on."

Monique allowed him to nudge her into the gym, but she gave her lips another vigorous rub.

The large square room was filled with the sounds of men laughing and balls bouncing on the hardwood floor. It was a full-sized basketball court with several rows of bleachers for spectators. There were about twelve people sitting to watch, most of them the wives or girlfriends of the players. She and Gary joined the six other members of their team, the Ravens, as they did a few minutes of warm-up drills.

"Let's pull it in!" demanded Sam, their captain. The six players surrounded him. "Okay, guys, let's go with the regular starters. Gary, I want you to stay on top of number 23. We need to shut down his three-pointers before he warms up."

Gary nodded.

"Nigel," Sam continued, firing off the instructions, "you cover number 19. Scott, take 3 and Evans . . ."

When he got to Monique's assignment, their eyes met briefly. Sam paused, and his brows lowered sharply as he scanned her face.

"Evans, you have 35. I'll take 20."

Monique nodded, wondering if she had imagined his momentary reaction. She brushed her hand over her lips again. Unfortunately, Sam was the type of guy who could easily make a woman stare at him so hard and imagine that he was looking back.

Everyone called him Sam or Samuels, but his full name was Tao Samuels. From what she understood, his father was African American and his mother was Chinese, so he had that striking, Tyson Beckford–thing going on, but with skin the color of golden caramel rather than dark chocolate. His face was long and angular, and he had piercing, intense eyes on an exotic slant and generously full lips. And if that weren't enough to remember him forever, Tao was blessed with a tall, lean frame and a natural grace and athleticism.

The ball game started a few minutes later. Though the league was technically for men, there was nothing in the rule books to prevent women from playing. So far, Monique was the only female to take advantage of the opportunity. She had joined the Ravens a few weeks earlier in September, and it did not take long for her ball skills to become obvious. She had played NCAA division basketball in college and was now the team's point guard, playing most of the game.

The opposing team, the Wild Dogs, was pretty good, but by the last couple of minutes in the game, it was clear that the Ravens were much better. This was the second time they had played each other, and the Ravens had won the first match-up by only a few points. Monique had been very new to the league at that time and had only played for a brief period. Tonight, with the flow of the game in her hands, the match was turning into a blow out, and the Wild Dogs were not taking the beating well.

In the last possession, like several times before, Monique dodged the man defending her and made a fast drive to the basket for a clear lay-up. The spectators on the bench were already snickering in anticipation of an embarrassingly easy play. But just as Monique leaped into the air with her arm extended, intending to roll the ball down the tips of her fingers, she felt a sudden impact against her legs, sending her careening wildly off balance.

It took all her effort and focus to keep her eyes on the basket, and as she headed for the hardwood, she watched the ball bounce around the rim before dropping in. *And one*, she exclaimed in her mind with victory. Then, she landed hard on her side with her left shoulder taking most of the jarring impact. Shouts of surprise and admiration filled the gym as the referee blew his whistle, indicating a foul. There were a few seconds of chaos before everyone realized that Monique was still on the ground and clearly injured.

Tao was the first to reach her, and she could hear the urgency in his voice and feel the warmth of his hand as he searched her legs for any fractures or sprains.

"Monique! Monique, are you okay?"

She squeezed her eyes tight, trying to fight the urge to scream at the pain that ran up from her collarbone to her neck. When she tried to answer him, she could not seem to suck any oxygen into her lungs.

"Monique!" added Gary as he crouched down near her head.

"I'm okay," she finally gasped. "My shoulder . . ."

"Don't move," Tao commanded as he shifted his attention to an area around her upper arm.

"It's okay," Monique told him in a stronger voice. "I just banged it."

"Stay still!" instructed Tao again.

She did as she was told and allowed him to gently inspect the area. He took his time, and Monique eventually opened her eyes to look up at him.

"Does that hurt?" he asked after prodding a tender spot and feeling her flinch.

Their eyes met, and Monique was taken aback by the intense concern reflected in his.

"Just a little," she whispered.

"Is she okay?" asked Gary.

The other guys on the team where surrounding them, all clearly anxious to hear how she was doing.

"I'm fine," Monique replied. "I just got the wind knocked out of me."

To assure them, she sat up slowly. Both Gary and Tao quickly took her arms and helped her to her feet. Monique could not help but wince at the movement in her bruised arm. Once she was seated on the bench, the referee blew his whistle again and the game resumed, with Tao taking her foul shot for her.

There were only six seconds left on the clock, enough time for a final possession by the Wild Dogs. But with the Ravens already winning by twenty-seven points, no one expected much to happen. The few spectators in the stands started to pack up their things, and Monique turned away from the court to grab her towel. By the time she turned back around, a fight had broken out on the court and both teams were yelling and pushing at each other.

Chapter 2

"Let go of me, Gary!" Tao demanded.

Gary had his arms wrapped around Tao's chest, forcibly pulling him away.

"Sam, man, just let it go," said Gary.

"I'm cool, I'm cool. It's over," replied Tao. His fists were clenched tight, ready to respond if provoked.

On the other side of the gym, a Wild Dog player was limping and cursing at Tao with every possible dirty word. The referee was standing between the two teams to ensure the conflict didn't escalate. Everyone else was standing still, wondering exactly what went down and waiting to see what would happen next. It took a few minutes, but the agitated Wild Dogs player was eventually led out of the room by his teammates.

"You tripped him on purpose, didn't you?" Gary asked after things had quieted down.

"Tsk! The idiot tripped over my foot," Tao told him.

"Yeah, sure he did."

"He's lucky I didn't shove my fist down his throat after what he did to Monique." Tao made this statement in a quiet, emotionless voice, but his face was hard with smothered fury. Gary nodded in agreement.

They both looked over at the bench as Monique touched her bruised shoulder and rolled it to check mobility and pain. Her oval face revealed a little discomfort, with slender, shapely lips pulled back and her even white teeth clenched hard.

Tao found his eyes drawn to her most dominant features: deep, smoky eyes, now surprisingly enhanced with a little makeup. They were one of the first things he had noticed when he had met Monique Evans over a month ago at the start of the basketball season. Even with her hair pulled back and in sweaty gym clothes, those eyes held the promise of sensuality. His first reaction was the natural male instinct to make a move. Then he saw her game skills, and any interest he felt was replaced with respect, almost admiration. Now, Tao tried to think of her as one of the guys.

"How does it feel?" Gary asked when they reached her.

"It's okay, just a little sore."

"You'll have to put some ice on it," Tao told her. She nodded, and the three of them made their way out of the now empty gym.

"Are we going to get something to eat?" asked Gary once they reached the men's locker room.

It was a routine for the three of them, and anyone else on the team who was free, to clean up then go to one of the nearby restaurants for dinner after the game.

"I think I'll pass, Coop," Monique told him.

"I'm out too," Tao added. He was about to explain why, when they were interrupted by a woman walking toward them from the front of the building.

"Tao, are you coming?"

The question was more like a command. She stopped behind him, and Tao didn't have to turn around to imagine the annoyed look on her face or the tight fist planted aggressively on her hip. His back straightened with annoyance.

"The game's been over for, like, twenty minutes or something. I've been just standing out here waiting."

"Hey, Tanisia, how are you?" Gary asked after several seconds passed and Tao did not respond to her.

"Okay, well, I'll see you guys later," Monique told them, clearly wanting to avoid the awkward situation. She turned and headed for the changing room. Gary took her cue and did the same.

"What's going on, Tao?"

"I don't know what you're talking about, Tanisia," he replied, finally turning around to face her.

"You don't know what I'm talking about? Do I look like an idiot?"

Tao could not contain the condescending smirk that spread on his lips. But, he managed not to say anything.

"What's going on between you and that chick?"

His brows lowered quickly, and his confusion was very obvious.

"What?"

"That chick," she uttered, pointing to the spot that Monique had just vacated. "What's going on? And, don't tell me that I imagined the way you looked at her!" demanded Tanisia, her voice getting louder with each sentence. "Then you go and attack the guy because he bumped into her. What the hell!"

Tao closed his eyes and let out a long breath, partly because her screeching was giving him a headache, but also because he didn't really know what to say. He had been really concerned about Monique and had let his anger get the better of him. But it was just because she was his teammate, right?

"Tanisia, I'm not talking to you while you're shouting in my face, all right? So, just calm down and stop being ridiculous. You're embarrassing me."

"Oh, please! I'm embarrassing you? How do you think I feel coming down here to watch your game, and you go to the rescue of some other woman? Then practically ignore me while I wait forever for you? And who do I find you talking to when you finally decide to show yourself?"

"Tanisia . . . !"

"You think you can treat me like this?"

She was a petite girl, maybe five feet, three inches, and no more than 110 pounds. Yet Tanisia had no problem getting up in his face with her finger wiggling under his nose. Her head shook and bobbed to enunciate every statement.

"Like I said," Tao replied, stressing his words and keeping his voice deadly quiet. "I don't know what you're going on about, and I'm not talking to you while you're shouting and getting on."

"Oh, so you're not going to answer me, huh?"

He looked her dead in the eyes to show how serious he was, then turned to walk away. Unfortunately, Monique chose that moment to step out of the changing room and was just in time to hear Tanisia blow her lid.

"Fine then! Walk away like you always do, you bastard! You better lose my number, 'cause there are plenty of men who want some of this! You ain't nothin', do you hear me? LOSE MY NUMBER!"

Tao's back was still turned to Tanisia, but from the corner of his eye, he could see Monique's expression, a mix of guilty curiosity, disgust, and humor as she watched Tanisia storm off, her high-heel boots clicking loudly on the tiled floors. Monique then gave him an assessing glance, as though seeing him for the first time, before also walking away.

Tao could only shake his head, wondering exactly what had happened to send this evening in such a weird direction.

Inside the men's changing room, Gary and a couple of other players were getting dressed after showering. The look on their faces made it obvious that everyone in the room had heard the confrontation.

"So I guess you're free to go get a meal, huh?" Gary asked before bursting into rolling, riotous laughter.

"Tsk! I don't know what's wrong with that girl," Tao said once his friend calmed down a little. "We've only been hanging for a few months. You'd think we were married or something."

"Who told you to invite her to the game? That's always a mistake."

"I didn't invite her! She invited herself, going on about where am I playing and why can't she come? I just got tired of hearing about it."

"Sam, my man, I've got to say, you knew her ass was a little crazy, but you went there anyway," stated Gary, chuckling again at his own words. "She's cute and all, but we're talking 'slash your tires,' 'boil your rabbit' crazy!"

Tao just gave him an annoyed glance then headed to the shower.

"How about Mexican? I'm craving tacos," Gary continued while still laughing.

Tao could still hear the guys ribbing him until he was standing under the spray of water. Now that the drama had passed, he could see the humor in the bizarre situation. His lips curved into a smile and he started to laugh silently.

Gary was right. Tao should have known that things would not work out between him and Tanisia. He had met her at the grocery store near his old apartment. They had both been picking out bunches of bananas, and their eyes had connected. He could tell right away that she was interested in him, just by the way she flipped her hair, and discreetly looked him up and down. Tao had not said anything to her at that moment, but gave in later when they passed each other twice in the frozen food aisle.

There was no doubt that Tanisia was an attractive girl. She had a tight, petite body and a nice, if not exactly pretty, face. But he had hesitated to make a move on her at first. She was a little too made up and obvious for his taste, wearing butt-hugging yoga pants and a tank top that clung to her torso like a second skin. She could have been coming from the gym, except she had on a full face of makeup.

When she finally spoke to him, he was standing near the ice-cream section, looking at the frozen desserts and trying to remember what he still had in his freezer.

"Excuse me? Have you seen any caramel crunch?"

Tao had not been surprised that she approached him. He had been anticipating it, but it still took him a few seconds to figure out what she was talking about. She must have mistaken his confused glance for flirtation, because she gave him a big smile and came several steps closer to him.

"I'm Tanisia," she added.

"Hey," he immediately replied. "I'm Tao."

"Tao?" she repeated, mispronouncing it. "That's interesting. Is it Spanish?"

It was the typical response he got to his foreign

name, so it didn't faze him. His face, skin tone, and particularly his eyes often had people confused about his nationality.

"No, it's Chinese," he explained.

"Really? You're Chinese?"

Tao almost smiled as she looked him up and down, her gaze lingering around his crotch as through trying to assess how Asian he really was.

"Half Chinese actually," was his brief response.

Tanisia just nodded, a sparkle in her eyes.

They spoke for a few minutes and eventually exchanged numbers. Things took a casual course after that, where they spoke a few times on the phone, and then went out to dinner. On the second date, Tanisia invited him back to her apartment and into her bed.

Though Tao wasn't dating anyone else at the moment, he had not considered their relationship to be exclusive or committed. Things between them were fine, and the sex was okay, but nothing more than that. It did not take long for him to realize that they had very little in common.

Clearly, after tonight's outrageous behavior it was over between them, and Tao wasn't at all upset about it. Her loud voice and unnecessary attitude had gotten tiresome really quick. She wasn't *that* cute.

Chapter 3

Monique had been playing organized basket-ball since junior high school and spent three years in college back in Michigan playing with the best and toughest girls in the country. She was accustomed to the bumps and bangs that came along with the sport and had been fortu-nate to avoid any serious injuries.

Despite how dramatic her fall had looked on Wednesday, there was very little harm done. The next day, her shoulder was uncomfortably stiff, with a sore spot that was tender to the touch. By Saturday, only a dark bruise was left on her upper arm.

Monique woke up that morning around eight o'clock as usual but lay snuggled under her com-forter for several minutes, letting her mind wander over the plans for the day. For the first time in weeks, she had a date. Unfortunately, it was a blind date arranged by her girlfriend Cara, and one that did not come with the best endorse-ment. "Very sweet" was the strongest term that

Cara had used to describe her coworker Colin Grant. Of course, Monique had flat-out refused at first, but then had to listen to a long lecture on how she needed to open up to new opportunities and possibilities. Finally, she agreed to the date just to shut Cara up.

According to her friend, Colin wanted to take her to dinner, but Monique wasn't going to be available until at least seven o'clock that evening. She had already promised to help Gary paint his house. In the end, Cara arranged for Monique to meet Colin for drinks at a lounge downtown at 8:00 PM.

Monique finally rolled out of bed about thirty minutes later. Gary wasn't expecting her at his house until around eleven o'clock, so she still had a couple of hours. She washed her face and brushed her teeth, then headed out the door for a walk, wearing cotton track pants and a windbreaker.

She lived in the Mission Bay area, an oceanfront community in the north end of San Diego. She was lucky enough to own a small bungalow less than a block from the beach. Unfortunately, Monique had purchased the house under the impression that Donald would move in with her once his separation was official. That never happened, and now she was stuck with a mortgage much higher than she was comfortable with. But, it was a nice house in a wonderful part of town, so she tried to make the best of it.

There had been several times in the last few months where Monique seriously considered selling the house because of the failure it represented, but the minute she hit the beach for one of her regular walks, she knew she could not do it. She had grown up in a Detroit suburb and had not even seen the ocean before moving to the West coast five years ago. Knowing she owned a piece of the California dream made her giddy with pleasure, regardless of how and why it happened.

Monique's walk took about forty-five minutes as she strolled along the boardwalk, then doubled back in the sand. Though it was only nine-thirty in the morning, there were lots of people around, mostly surfers and permanent residents enjoying the beach before the tourists descended. The coastal weather in late October was fairly cool, but that did not stop natives and visitors from enjoying the endless sunshine.

Once back home, Monique quickly jumped into the shower. She then pulled on track pants and an oversized T-shirt, old and worn, appropriate for a day of messy painting. Her shoulder-length hair was pulled into a casual ponytail. She was all set to leave her bedroom but then stopped to look at herself in the large dressing mirror on the wall.

The image reflected there was of an athletic woman, slightly taller than average, with a slender frame now hidden behind baggy sweats. It was a picture that Monique used to be comfortable with, maybe even one she sometimes hid behind. But now, she just looked sloppy and unkempt, like a girl who was afraid to show her beauty and femininity.

She let out a deep sigh. Her relationship with Donald had helped her see that.

They had met at work about four years ago, at least six months before they had started seeing each other. Monique had been very new at Sector Asset and it was her second job after her MBA. She was working in the sales department as an analyst, and Donald Sanderson was one of their new clients.

That summer, they spent quite a bit of time together but mostly in the work environment. There were a couple of group dinners where they had the opportunity to talk on a more personal level, but that was all. At the time, Monique found him interesting and attractive, but he was older and married, so she had not thought about it beyond that. Now, looking back with more experienced eyes, she could see that Donald had been flirting with her and checking out her interest in him from the beginning.

He had taken another job sometime in the fall, but they met again at a party in January of the following year. Monique and a few of her work colleagues were out celebrating a big win at a bar near the office. She had not noticed Donald among the Friday evening crowd, but he made a point of approaching her as she got ready to leave the bar. They chatted only for a few minutes, but long enough for him to confirm that she was still with Sector Asset. On Monday morning, there was an e-mail from him suggesting they get together for drinks.

Monique often wondered what it was about

Donald that caused her to respond to his advances. Flattery? Curiosity? He had been thirty-nine years old at the time, fairly average-looking but very polished and well-dressed. He was also fourteen years older than Monique and refreshingly mature and sophisticated.

Of course, there was his charm and persuasiveness, then his incredible ability to lie and manipulate so convincingly. Those were the qualities that got her to stay in a destructive relationship with a married man long after the explanations about a separation and impending divorce could be still be believable.

Monique sighed deeply again while still inspecting her reflection. There was no viable alternative for her hair other than the practical ponytail, but she changed out of the dingy sweats into figure-hugging jeans and a pretty white cotton shirt with short, capped sleeves and tailored pleats over the stomach. She then threw the large T-shirt and track pants into a duffle bag along with a few toiletry items, and headed out the door.

Gary lived about fifteen minutes away in a low, ranch-style house on a quiet cul-de-sac. Monique pulled into the empty driveway and paused for a few seconds before shutting off her car. It was several minutes after eleven o'clock, but there was no sign of Gary or his dark blue Lincoln. She pulled out her cell phone to check for any missed calls, but there weren't any. *Where could he be?*

Monique was about to dial his cell phone number when a sharp knock on her car window caused her to jump. Her eyes were wide with surprise as she looked up to find Tao Samuels bent low looking back at her. His face was flushed and his skin was damp with sweat. It took her a few seconds to realize that he was trying to talk to her, and she finally lowered the driver-side window.

"Have you been waiting long?" asked Tao.

"No, I just got here," Monique explained. "Where's Gary?"

"At the hardware store, I think. But he should be back soon," he explained as he stepped back and opened her door. "He needed new brushes and a few other things."

Monique grabbed her duffle bag, then stepped out of the car. Tao was already walking up the driveway, so she followed him. As she approached his back, she could see that his black nylon shirt was dripping with sweat and sticking to his back. It was obvious that he had been out running.

She followed him into the house and closed the door behind her. Standing in the entranceway, she continued to watch Tao's back as he walked down the hall leading to the bedrooms, casually pulling off his wet top along the way. His broad shoulders tapered down to narrow hips and hard, square glutes that were barely concealed beneath the low waistband of his loose shorts.

"There's some fresh coffee in the kitchen,"

Tao had turned suddenly to make the statement, catching Monique by surprise while her eyes were still fastened on the lower half of his body. He disappeared into the bathroom before she could respond, or even close her mouth. She heard him turn on the shower a few seconds later.

Monique took advantage of his offer and poured herself a cup of coffee. She should not have been surprised to find Tao there. Gary had mentioned a few weeks ago that the renovations on Tao's new condo were delayed. The lease on his rental expired, so he needed to crash at Gary's for about a month in between.

Gary finally arrived about fifteen minutes later and two of their other friends, Jason and Isaac, arrived soon after. The five of them quickly got to work painting the living room, kitchen, and main hallway of Gary's cozy 1950s house. Monique was given the task of taping off the trim while the men covered and moved the furniture, then patched and sanded holes in the wall.

Once they got into a rhythm, the conversation among the guys become pretty lively. Jason started telling the others about the get-together he and Isaac had gone to the night before. As usual, Monique listened to their antics quietly, always surprised at how much grown men gossiped. From what she could decipher, it had been a party for a girl they all knew named Josephine.

"Gary, man, you should have been there," Jason admonished. "Her roommate, Leanne, kept asking for you all night!"

Gary just shrugged.

"Ah, forget it, Jason," Isaac threw in with a devilish grin. "You know Leanne is not his type."

"Yeah, that right. She has a job and real breasts!" replied Jason.

They all laughed except for Gary who just rolled his eyes. Monique had to chuckle too because Jason's observation was pretty close to the truth. For whatever reason, Gary seemed to always find the most simple, fake women out there. And no matter how hard his friends tried to make him see the disastrous pattern, he just ignored them.

"She's just not my type, that's all," Gary finally replied.

"We know your type," added Tao in a voice dripping with sarcasm.

"Seriously, though, Gary," Isaac said. "I don't understand the way you think. Leanne is smart, stable, and pretty cute. You keep talking about finding that special woman to settle down and have kids with, but then you make a beeline for the first broke, hoodrat you see. I'm not saying don't hit it where you can get it, but you can't turn a booty call into a wife, if you know what I'm saying."

"You guys don't know what you're talking about. I know that Noreen was a mistake, but . . ." stated Gary, trying hard not to sound defensive.

"Mistake? Brother, she had two kids ten months apart for two brothers! I mean, biological brothers! Is that even physically possible? Come on now!" Jason spat with obvious disgust.

"They were eighteen months apart," Gary clarified.

"Oh, my mistake."

The others laughed uproariously.

"Oh, forget ya'll!" cursed Gary, and stalked off to the bathroom.

His friends cackled even harder.

"Samuels, Tanisia was there last night," Jason stated once things calmed down.

"Really," he replied, but his tone revealed very little interest.

"Yeah. And after a couple of drinks, she was all over Big Mike. I take it you guys are done?"

Big Mike was Josephine's older brother. They called him that because he was at least six feet, four inches, and built like linebacker.

"Pretty much," Tao confirmed in a quiet voice. "She's a little too crazy for me."

"See, that's what I'm talking about! You and Gary have got to stop messing with these young girls. They're nothing but drama," Jason replied. "I'm telling you, find yourself a mature woman who knows what she wants."

Gary returned in time to hear Jason's advice.

"You mean, like some hungry cougar? That's just not my style, man," he replied, shaking his head.

"It has nothing to do with age, Gary," explained Jason. "I'm talking about someone who's not all caught up in finding Mr. Right to take care of her bills, get married, and have the 2.5 kids. Someone who's just looking for a friend that can take care of her plumbing, and that's it, if you know what I mean."

"Yeah, right!" scoffed Gary. "If you're talking about Josephine, then you better forget it. That bitch is going to get you killed, 'cause her husband's a Navy Seal. Tao will tell you. They were stationed together a few years ago. You can guarantee that he would hunt you down, and no one would ever find your body."

"Naw, I'm not talking about Josephine or married women either. Trust me, there are lots of beautiful, successful women who don't want a man in their lives except for some good loving."

"Yeah? So where are they and how come I've never met one?" Isaac asked.

"I just told you, you guys are too busy chasing after these young, ripe college girls. Right, Monique?"

Monique had just finished her taping, and was rolling her shoulder to relieve a little stiffness still there. She had only been listening to the conversation with half an ear.

"What?" she asked now that all four men were staring at her expectantly.

"Wouldn't you be interested in a relationship with a man that was strictly about fulfilling your sexual needs?" Jason repeated.

She could only look at him, uncertain of the context of the question.

"I'm just saying," he continued. "You're a busy, successful woman. And you're always complaining about not having time in your life for a relationship. Maybe you just need a friend with benefits."

Monique realized that Jason wasn't talking about her specifically, just other women like her. She shrugged and gave him a wicked grin.

"There would have to be some pretty awesome benefits!"

They all laughed and went back to their painting tasks, and Jason continued his lecture.

"I'm telling you guys, it's time to elevate your game," he stated.

"Yeah, right!" Isaac interjected. "These women may say they want only a sexual friendship, but I guarantee within a few months, they'll be talking about love and commitment. And the better you lay the pipe, the faster they will fall. They're just not wired for casual sex like men are."

"That's not true," Monique replied.

Gary and Isaac looked at her with surprise, while Jason nodded, welcoming her contribution to the argument. Tao's expression was unreadable.

"Some women can really have an honest, mutually satisfying sexual relationship without falling in love," she explained. "There will probably be some feelings there for her partner, but there is nothing wrong with that. It doesn't automatically mean she's going to change her mind and want to get married and everything. And I guarantee you that if she's putting it on him right, he's the one who will be begging her for the commitment!"

They all laughed, and the debate continued for several more minutes. Gary and Isaac were clearly unconvinced that such women actually existed. Tao remained silent, but when his eyes met Monique's again, there was a new light in their depths.

Chapter 4

The group of friends was finished painting Gary's place earlier than expected. They ordered a couple of pizzas for dinner, and Monique was back home before six-thirty that evening. She immediately went into the shower to get ready for her date. She was still not excited about meeting Colin Grant, but it was too late to back out. While in the shower, she created a plan to spend about an hour with him, then make up an excuse about having a headache, or something, then head home early. If he turned out to be pleasant company, then she might stay a little longer, but the possibility seemed very unlikely to Monique. There had been very few men in her life that she found both intellectually interesting and physically attractive.

The timing worked out well, and Monique pulled her car into the parking lot of the restaurant with a couple of minutes to spare. Colin was to be waiting for her at the front entrance, but none of the few men around met his description.

She decided to take a quick look inside in case she had misunderstood the arrangements.

Despite her reluctance at meeting someone new, Monique still chose to put some effort into her appearance. She knew she looked good, but it still felt nice to see the men look at her with appreciation and interest as she made her way through the crowded bar. She wore a sleeveless black cotton tunic with a simple boat neckline in the front and a plunging, scalloped back that left her skin bare right down to the base of her spine. She had paired it with long white shorts that ended around her knees and accentuated the long length of her legs. Her feet were clad in silver stiletto heels, about three inches high, bringing her to almost five feet, ten inches tall.

She was headed back to the front entrance when a guy stepped through the door and looked around as though searching for someone. Monique indentified Colin right away from the picture that Cara had e-mailed her, and she walked toward him. He smiled widely when he recognized her.

"Hi, Colin," she said graciously while extending her hand. "I'm Monique."

"Hey, Monique," he replied warmly, shaking her hand with a surprisingly strong and confident grip. "I hope you haven't been waiting long?"

"Not at all. Just a few minutes."

"Good. So, should we get a table or just sit at the bar?" he asked while looking around at the Saturday evening crowd that was steadily growing.

"There were a couple of free tables near the back of the bar," she suggested.

"Okay," Colin replied easily, then indicated for her to go first.

As soon as they took their seats in a small booth, a waitress approached them and took their orders for red wine.

"So, Cara tells me that you guys have known each other since public school. Back in Detroit, right? That's pretty interesting," commented Colin.

"Yeah, we've been best friends since we were seven years old. Her family moved to San Diego right after our sophomore year in high school. I moved out here to finish my degree."

"What did you take?"

"My undergrad was in Economics at the University of Michigan, then I got my MBA at San Diego State."

"And you're in sales, right?" he asked.

"That's right."

There was a small pause as they looked at each other while sipping at the wine. Monique used that time to look at him more closely. She had to admit that Colin was much better looking in real life. He had an average sort of face with pleasant features, a clean shaven and neat appearance, with his hair cut low. There wasn't really anything remarkable about him, except his personality was much more vibrant than she had anticipated. Her interest was piqued a little bit.

"So, how long have you known Cara?" she finally asked.

Colin laughed a little.

"Only a few weeks, actually. I started working at the real estate firm at the end of September."

"Really?" replied Monique with obvious surprise. Cara had been bugging her to meet Colin for almost that long!

"Yeah. We just hit it off right away. She's a really great person," Colin stated, still grinning. "I think she mentioned setting us up on my second day at work."

"No way!" Monique exclaimed. "She did not!"

Colin laughed again while nodding. "Yup! Apparently, I'm perfect for you, and exactly the type of guy you should be going out with. You should listen to her. She is pretty perceptive."

Monique could only bury her face in her hands, completely embarrassed and appalled by her friend's portrayal of her as desperate. Cara had made it seem as though she knew Colin well and had worked with him for a long time. Monique silently vowed to kill her.

"What else did Cara tell you about me?" she finally asked once she'd regained her composure.

"Not much. She definitely did not tell me how gorgeous you are."

His once charming smile now seemed a little sly and cocky. Monique's interest started a quick decline toward nonexistent. She was about to say something sharply sarcastic, to bring him down a notch, but their waitress chose that moment to stop by to check on them.

"So, tell me everything there is to know about Monique Evans," Colin continued.

Monique had to try really hard not to roll her eyes. Did he really think his lines were original? Or did Cara's aggressive matchmaking portray Monique as naïve as well as pathetic?

"Well, there's not much to tell," she finally replied. "What about you? How long have you been working in real estate?"

As she suspected, Colin had no problem talking about himself, and he did not need much prompting to get rolling.

"But that's just my day job," he told her with a dismissive shrug, after spending a good twenty minutes telling her all about being a high-end real estate broker in San Diego. "My real passion is my poetry."

"Really?" she replied on cue, barely able to suppress a yawn.

"Maybe you've heard some of my stuff. I go by the name Soulistic?" He didn't wait for her response before busting into a rhyme. "Sister girl . . . baby girl. . . . Where were you when I tongued my first kiss? When I stole my first feel? When I bust my first nut? *(dramatic pause)* Sister girl, the first and last was all about you . . . baby girl, it was all about you. Your scent, your feel was always in my mind, heart, and senses. Waiting for your essence to appear in my world. Sister girl, where were you until today?"

It took Monique a good ten seconds to process his words. She wasn't a big fan of poetry or spoken word, but she recognized the style of his rhyming, with dramatic enunciations and word emphasis. It didn't sound too bad.

"That was "Baby Girl," one of my more well-known verses."

She nodded in response, then he went right into another poem, then two more after that. Monique didn't know if she should laugh at his act of intense sensitivity and passion, or just work on getting her hand out from the grasp of his fingers.

"Wow," she replied. "That was . . . great!"

She finally pulled her hand away to pick up her wine glass.

"Thank you. Maybe you can come out to hear me perform sometime. I do events all over the city and on the radio. But next year will be bigger and better. I already have a couple of gigs booked in LA for January. Soulistic is on the rise."

Oh, no! He did not just refer to himself in the third person, Monique thought. It was time to cut this off and put the guy out of his misery.

"Sorry, Colin, I have to run to the bathroom." She stood up, then reached into her purse and pulled out fifteen dollars. "This is for my drink in case the waitress comes by."

She walked away before he could respond or react.

Monique didn't actually need to use the facilities, she just wanted an excuse to end Colin's self-absorbed chatting, especially before he started rhyming again. But, while there, she used the opportunity to wash her hands and freshen up her makeup. As she walked back to their table, she braced herself for the inevitable gentle but firm letdown. She stopped beside his chair but did not sit back down.

"Hey there," he said, grinning up at her with charm and confidence.

"Colin, it was nice meeting you," she replied with a polite but distant smile. She stuck out her hand to silently say good-bye.

He was clearly confused for a few seconds, looking back and forth from her face to her still-extended hand.

"Oh. Oh, all right," he eventually replied as he stood up also. "You have to get going."

"No, I'm going to finish my wine. But, again it was good to meet you."

Monique then sat in her chair and occupied herself by looking through her purse. It was a clear message that the date was over. Out of the corner of her eye, she could see a few different expressions pass over his face, including insulted and finally a little anger. It took him a few minutes, but eventually Colin nodded a bit and walked away.

Monique almost felt guilty about blowing him off, but it was his own fault for being so cocky and egotistical. They had spent only about an hour together, and it was very obvious that his favorite topic was Colin . . . or Soulistic. She couldn't begin to waste her time on someone like that. Clearly, Cara was very wrong about the type of men that Monique should be dating!

As she had planned, Monique finished her wine while sitting alone and looking around at all the people socializing on a Saturday night.

There was a pretty even mix of men and women. Some were clearly on dates, but most looked like they were in groups just having a good time. She spent a few minutes trying to remember the last time she felt like part of that single and carefree crowd, dressed up in funky, sexy clothes and flirting easily.

Monique had never been that girl. She had always been too focused on a goal or objective, like finishing school or advancing in her career, to be frivolous with her time. Donald had often commented that her seriousness and maturity was one of the things that attracted him to her, despite her age. At the time, flushed with pleasure from his praise, she considered it a positive thing. Now, sitting alone and surrounded by youthful cheerfulness, she felt only ancient and depleted of joy.

Monique ended up staying for about an extra fifteen minutes before finally leaving the bar. She had just exited from the front doors when a taxi pulled into the driveway of the restaurant, and she stepped out of its path to continue on to her car. A few steps later, she heard her name yelled out by a deep, male voice, so she stopped in her tracks to turn around.

"Monique!"

There was Tao Samuels as he closed the door of the cab, surrounded by two women and another guy. He stepped away from his companions to approach her.

"Hey, Samuels," she said, a little breathless with surprise.

"Hey, are you leaving?" he asked.

"Uh . . . yeah. I had just met someone for drinks, so I'm heading home."

"So early? What's the rush? Why don't you stay and hang out for a bit?" he suggested easily.

Monique looked past his shoulder to the trio of friends waiting patiently for him under the lights of the restaurant entrance.

"Thanks for the invite, but five might mean a crowd if you're here on a double date, don't you think?" she asked with a teasing smile.

Tao smiled back.

"Nah, it's not like that. Come. At least stay for a drink or two," he coaxed.

Monique could not think of a reason to turn down his offer. It wasn't like there was anything waiting for her at home except laundry.

"Okay," she finally assented.

"All right. Hey guys, this is Monique Evans," he announced to his friends. "She plays on my basketball team. Monique, this is Anthony and his wife, Darlene. And this is Anthony's sister, Vanessa. Anthony and I were in the service together."

Monique smiled at each of them while shaking each of their hands. "Nice to meet you all," she added.

Once inside, the group decided to wait for a table in the main dining room rather than take their chances over by the bar. They were seated about five minutes later and spent the time exchanging some information between Monique and the other three. She discovered that Anthony was still in the military but had recently been promoted to a domestic role within the Ministry of Defense. This night out was to celebrate his new position away from combat.

"So, you two play basketball together?" asked Darlene.

They had been seated in a booth. Anthony sat between his wife and sister on one side, while Tao and Monique were on the other. They had received their drink orders and were waiting for a few appetizers to arrive.

"Yeah," Tao confirmed. "Monique is our star player."

The others smiled and looked at her.

"Hardly," she piped in. "You guys are just surprised that a girl can play as well as any of you men."

"Honestly, that's what I thought at first," Tao replied, turning slightly so that he was looking right at her. "Gary mentioned recruiting you, but didn't exactly tell us how good you were."

Monique looked down at the table, unable to find any words to respond with. She wasn't shy about her ball skills. It was the heat of Tao's eyes focused intently on hers that made her flushed and befuddled.

"Monique played NCAA ball in college," he continued, turning back to face his friends across the table. "Won two national championships, right?"

Their eyes met again briefly. Monique took a drink of her rum and Coke before shrugging nonchalantly.

"It was a long time ago," she added.

"Wow, that's pretty impressive!" commented

Anthony. "I've played with Tao a few times over the years, and he's pretty good. If he's impressed with your skills, you must pretty amazing."

"She is."

Maybe it was the mix of rum with the red wine she had earlier, but Monique was starting to feel a little-lightheaded and susceptible to the heat of Tao's gaze on her again. It stirred up a tingle at the base of her stomach. She took another long sip of her drink, resisting the urge to meet his eyes again.

Chapter 5

The five of them stayed at the restaurant for another couple of hours, nibbling on their appetizers and enjoying a second round of drinks. They laughed and talked about a variety of subjects, including tales about both the guys during their years in the military. Anthony was a great storyteller, and he did most of the talking while Tao occasionally added a few comments here and there.

Monique was the most silent of them, seemingly happy to listen to the others bantering back and forth. At first, her quietness had Tao wondering if she was uncomfortable being thrown into an evening with his friends, but she eventually relaxed and seemed to be having a good time just observing the rest of them.

It was a few minutes after midnight when the two men took care of the check and the group made its way out of the restaurant, now almost empty of people. Tao was behind Monique and noticed that she seemed a little unsteady on her feet. Not drunk, but maybe a little tipsy. He instinctively put a guiding hand on her lower back, his fingers brushing the naked skin exposed by her provocative top. She paused for a moment and looked back at him, appearing confused by his touch.

"Are you okay?" he asked her.

Monique blinked with a lazy smile on her face. Tao smiled back, amused by the fact that she was definitely a little inebriated.

"Hmm . . . I think that last drink went right to my head," she whispered, now looking sheepish and slightly embarrassed.

"Did you drive? I'll drive you home," he offered after she nodded yes.

"Are you sure?" she asked.

"Yeah, I barely touched my second beer."

"Okay," Monique accepted with another smile, clearly relieved and grateful. "But how will you get home?"

He shrugged, unconcerned.

"I'll take a cab from your place."

"Okay," she said again. "Thanks, Tao."

They continued walking out the exit, and it struck Tao that it was the first time he had heard her use his first name. He liked the way it sounded.

When they caught up to Anthony and the girls, there was already a cab ready for them. Tao explained that he would be driving Monique home.

"You're in Mission Bay, right?" Tao asked once they were driving out of the parking lot.

"Hmm hmm," she confirmed. "You can take the I-5 to I-8, and I'll direct you from there."

"That's a great neighborhood. How long have you lived there?"

"Not long, just since spring. It was always my dream to live near the beach, but things didn't turn out the way I had planned." Tao gave her a questioning glance, silently asking her to explain more. "I bought the house expecting that my fiancé at the time would move in soon after. Well, I guess he wasn't really my fiancé. I don't think you can actually be engaged to someone who is still married and living with his wife. Yeah, I know. Stupid, huh? I was in a relationship with a married man and actually believed he was leaving her."

Tao was a little taken aback and not sure how to respond. Monique just did not seem like the type of woman who would end up in that kind of a situation. As far as he could see, she was very smart and very successful, completely lacking the insecurities and gullibility that he would expect of a woman who would fall into such a trap.

"We were together for more than three years, if you can believe it," she added, almost as though she sensed the questions he wanted to ask. "And, yes, I knew he was married when we met. But he claimed that they were technically separated but stayed in the house because they could not agree on whether it should be sold. Or, that was one of the excuses anyway."

He glanced over at her to make sure she was okay. Surprisingly, Monique seemed more amused than upset.

"Anyway," she continued, dragging out the word dramatically. "The house is much bigger than I need for just myself, and it was a little lonely at first. But now, I just can't bring myself to seriously consider selling it."

"That makes sense," Tao said. "Properties in that area are hard to come by."

"Exactly. And everything happens for a reason, right?"

"Right," he concurred.

"Right. Everything happens for a reason," she repeated like a mantra.

They were silent for a few minutes. Monique was looking out the window while Tao focused on his driving.

"You're moving into your new place soon, right?" she finally asked.

"Yeah, in a couple weeks."

"So, I guess that means you plan to stay in San Diego for a while?"

Tao knew immediately what she was referring to. Right at the beginning of the ball season, while they were having dinner after a game, he had told both Monique and Gary that he wasn't sure how long he would stay in the city. It was just before he had bought his new apartment, and while he was still feeling out his current contract in civilian surveillance and security consulting. But everything had fallen into place soon after, and he was now pretty content with living in San Diego for the foreseeable future.

"Yeah, I think so. It's as good a place as any for now."

"You don't have any family here?" she asked.

"No. My mom lives in Bakersfield."

"No other family?"

"Nope," he replied. "I'm an only child, and I'm not sure where my father is. There are a few cousins floating around, but none that I'm particularly close to."

They were about to get off Interstate 8 on the south end of Mission Bay. Monique spent the next few minutes giving Tao more detailed directions to her house. He pulled the car into her driveway shortly afterward.

"Thanks again for driving me home, Tao," she told him before she opened the passenger door and stepped out.

"No problem at all."

He exited the car also, and walked with her to the front door.

"I don't usually drink that much. . . . I don't feel that drunk or anything . . . just a little fuzzy maybe."

Monique smiled up at him again, her eyes shining with a mix of embarrassment and self-consciousness. Tao smiled back and handed her the key ring. She fumbled in the dark, obviously trying to find the house keys. His smile widened with amusement, then he took them out of her hands and easily slid the door key into the lock.

"Thanks," she mumbled. "I'll call a cab for you."

He stood in the front hall while she walked further into the house and stepped into what he assumed was the kitchen. Tao heard her on the phone for a few seconds then she was back.

"Okay, they should be here in about ten minutes. Do you want something to drink? A glass of water or something?" she offered.

Tao had not really thought past getting Monique home safely. Sure, he had immediately noticed how hot she looked that night, with her bare back exposed and the thrust of her uncovered breasts teasing the fabric of her top. He had even had the chance to admire the sexy length of her legs in her very high heels. But, it had only been a natural appreciation of a beautiful woman. Not once had he really thought about holding her or kissing her. But now, standing just inside her house while she looked up at him with eyes more open and honest than ever before, her lips slightly parted, it was all he could think about.

"I wouldn't mind a glass of water," he told her.

Monique didn't move, and Tao didn't hesitate to pull her close with a gentle hand behind her head. He placed his mouth on hers. It started out as a simple kiss, meant to test her interest in something more. But the second he brushed his lips across hers, it felt like pure electricity. Tao pulled back in surprise, hovering only an inch from her, trying to understand the jolt that hit him somewhere below his navel. Then, he kissed her again with no questions or hesitation.

Everything around them faded away until all that was left was the taste and feel of her mouth. Tao swept his lips across hers, taking his time to travel from one corner to the other. Her lips were soft and silky, enticing him to continue nibbling and sucking on them. His tongue teased the inside edge of her mouth, sweeping across its plumb wetness.

On and on the kiss went, with Tao's hands cupping Monique's face and his fingers teasing her cheeks. Then, she opened her mouth and swept her tongue along his. It was an incredibly erotic touch, and Tao sucked in a sharp breath. They both paused for a moment, as though acknowledging that the temperature between them was about to get hotter.

When their mouths connected again, the kiss was open, deep, and wet. Tao pulled her closer until their bodies were fused. Their tongues brushed and stroked with growing hunger. One of his hands swept down her smooth, sculpted back to rest at the base of her spine. Monique reached her arms to drape them over his shoulders. A deep moan escaped her throat. His body reacted immediately.

Tao had been so totally engrossed in the heat of their touch that he had forgotten everything else, including the fact that Monique was a friend and more than a little tipsy. But while her gasp of pleasure raised his blood pressure, it also forced him back to reality. Monique's reaction to their kisses might not be so heated if she were completely sober. And she may not feel so good about things in the morning.

As much as Tao was enjoying their kisses and wanting more, the idea of taking advantage of her current state did not sit well with him. He stole a couple more hot kisses, pulling her tongue into his mouth for one final brush. Then, he pulled away slowly. It took Monique a few seconds to realize what had happened. When she finally opened her eyes to look up at him, they were smoky and heavy-hooded. They said that she was still wrapped up in the arousal between them.

It would have been so easy for Tao to kiss her again and lead them both to her bedroom, but he resisted. It took almost all his strength. A horn sounded outside at that moment, announcing the arrival of his cab. The timing was perfect.

"I better get going," he told her in a soft voice.

Monique looked down at the floor but didn't say anything.

"Are you feeling okay?" he then asked.

"I'm fine," she replied while nodding.

"Okay. Drink lots of water before you go to bed, okay?"

She smiled, finally meeting his eyes.

"I will."

Tao intended to just walk out the door, but he could not resist one last soft kiss. The same electricity shot through him again, leaving him a little dazed. He quickly left her house a few seconds later, the taste of her like a stain on his lips.

Chapter 6

Other than a tinge of embarrassment, Monique woke up the next morning feeling very little effects from her night of overindulgence. She had drunk more than she usually did, and had definitely been tipsy, but she easily remembered everything from the night before. Everything, except what exactly had caused her and Tao Samuels to start kissing next to her front door.

She rolled over on the bed to look up at the ceiling.

Monique could not remember anything but looking up at him and wishing he would stay for more than just a glass of water. Then his hands and mouth were on her and it was better than anything she could have imagined.

Had she kissed him, or had he reached out to her? It really should not matter at this point, but Monique hoped that she had not jumped all over him like a sloppy lush! She would like to think that Tao had been secretly wanting her for weeks and could not resist any longer.

She smiled to herself at how silly her imagination could be.

Yes, there was no question that she had found Tao incredibly attractive. Who wouldn't? But he wasn't her type. He was way too beautiful for his own good and definitely a bit of a ladies man. The few times they had hung out, she had always found him funny and easygoing, but something told her that wasn't how he was with his women. And there appeared to be a constant string of them.

Monique finally got out of bed and went directly to the shower. Cara and her family were expecting her for breakfast in a couple of hours. She was ready in about twenty-five minutes, then spent another half an hour putting a few loads of laundry in the washer and doing some sweeping up.

Cara lived only about fifteen minutes away from Monique, up in La Jolla, but she made a quick stop to pick up a bag of Cara's favorite coffee beans and some fresh fruit to add to their breakfast. She arrived at her friend's house a few minutes after 10:00 AM.

Monique remembered the first time she had driven up to La Jolla to visit Cara and her young family. It was about three months after Monique had moved to San Diego, and she was still pretty unfamiliar with the city. She knew that Cara had married a successful plastic surgeon and lived in a nice area, but Monique had been completely unprepared for what she found. The homes gradually got bigger and more elaborate as she got closer to the address. When she finally reached the house, Monique found a large Spanish-style home with a three-car garage and elaborate manicured gardens. She checked the number on the door three times before she rang the doorbell.

Now, five years later, the sight of the beautiful property still caused Monique's breath to catch. She pulled into the driveway and grabbed the bag of food and coffee before heading around the side of the house to the backyard. There she found Cara setting the table out on the patio, a stunning view of the Pacific Ocean as a backdrop. Her youngest daughter, Meghan, was in her high chair, banging away with a set of spoons.

"Auntie Monique! You're here!"

The shout came from just inside one of the four French doors that ran across the back of the house. A second later, Monique's first goddaughter, Madison, was running toward her and enthusiastically wrapped her arms around Monique's waist with a tight hug.

"Hey, Pooky!" Monique replied, using the nickname for Madison that she had used since the day she was born. "Do you want to help Auntie with these things?"

"Sure! I'll take the fruit. It looks delicious. The mangoes are my favorite, you know."

Maddie was only four and a half years old, but somewhere along the line, she had picked up a vocabulary far beyond her years. Monique always marveled at her ability to communicate with adults as though she was one of them.

"You know what?" Monique replied while

keeping the fruit tray away from her eager hands. "Why don't you take this bag instead? It's much lighter and it's for mommy. And I promise you can still have all the mangoes you want."

Maddie reluctantly took the paper bag. She then sniffed the aromatic contents. Her eyes sparkled with recognition.

"Mommy, Auntie Monique brought you your favorite coffee! Chocolate-flavored coffee, right, Auntie Monique?"

"Your are too smart, Pooky!"

"Not really," replied Maddie. "You always bring mommy flavored coffee."

She then walked away carrying the gift bag into the kitchen, leaving Monique feeling put in her place.

"Hey, babe!" Cara said when Monique approached the patio table.

The two old friends hugged tight. Cara was only about five feet, two inches, in her bare feet. Even wearing a pair of high platform wedge shoes, she was still a couple of inches shorter than Monique. The differences did not stop there. Both women were a similar shade of smooth chestnut, but while Monique wore her dark brown hair bone straight from a perm, Cara had hers cut low to the scalp to reveal her tight natural curls.

"Hey. How are you doing?" Monique asked. "How is Meghan feeling? Does she still have that cold?"

Meghan was eighteen months old and she stopped banging as soon as she heard her name. She then gave Monique a toothy grin.

"She's much better. It was probably just a bit of teething," Cara replied. "Thanks for the coffee, by the way."

The two women went into the kitchen to gather the rest of the breakfast. Cara had a housekeeper and nanny named Theresa who lived with them during the week but had the weekends off. Since Cara didn't have to cook most of the time, she liked to go all out on Sundays. On the counter, there were containers already filled with scrambled eggs, bacon, waffles, and hash-browned potatoes. A pot of coffee was already brewed, and there was a jug of freshly squeezed orange juice.

"Where's Kyle and Melissa?" asked Monique as they carried the food outside.

Kyle Spencer was Cara husband of six years. They had met when Cara was in her second year at the university and Kyle was in his last year of medical school. Now he was building a very successful plastic surgery practice that serviced the rich and famous in southern California. But Kyle was also world renowned for his work to correct rare deformities, often done pro bono.

Melissa Drummond was Cara's younger sister.

"He's in his office, but I'm sure he'll be out soon" Cara told her. "Mel should be here already. She called this morning to say she was bringing someone with her."

"Really? Who?"

Cara was about to respond when Kyle stepped out onto the patio. Meghan squealed with delight, chanting "daddy, daddy, daddy" at the top of her lungs with her arms outstretched. There was no mistaking the similarities between father and daughter. They both had the same dark cocoa skin and large, oval eyes. Meghan's face still had the roundness of a toddler, but it was clear that she would end up with a strong square jaw and her chin had the clear indentation of a cleft that matched her dad's.

Kyle immediately took her out of the high chair. He then gave Monique a welcoming hug. Melissa arrived a couple of minutes later, followed closely by her new boyfriend whom she introduced as just "Jones." He nodded to everyone around the table with a casual upswing of his chin, and no further explanation was given about whether Jones was his first or last name. Cara and Monique looked at each other, trying not to laugh. Melissa was twenty-four years old and seemed perpetually attracted to men from the hard-knock life.

Ten minutes later, the group, including Madison, were seated around the table enjoying the meal that Cara had put together. Jones was telling Kyle about his job as a security guard while Mel listened in. It left the two friends free to have their own conversation, and it wasn't long before Cara brought up Monique's date with Colin the night before.

"So, how did it go?"

Monique's facial expression was enough to indicate it had not gone well.

"Okay, what happened?" Cara eventually asked.

"Nothing happened. He's just not my type. He

was nice enough, but. . . . Well, let's just say that we had nothing in common."

"Really? I'm surprised! Colin is so smart, confident, and well dressed. I was sure you guys would hit it off," explained Cara, clearly disappointed.

"He seemed fine at first, even after he told me how you had described me as desperately single!" Monique replied, shooting her a burning glare. "And I admit that he was attractive. But then he started talking about being a spoken-word artist and referring to himself in the third person! Let's just say confidence quickly turned to arrogance. He just went on and on about himself."

"Really? I had no clue."

"Yeah. Then he proceeded to recite a string of his rhymes for me. I like poetry as much as the next girl, but I just have no interest in dating someone like that. He was just a little too intense and self-involved for me. I have heard enough pretty words to last me a lifetime."

"So, how did it end?"

"Well, I put the money on the table for my drink and told him it was nice meeting him. But, I made it clear that I didn't feel a connection."

"He let you pay for your drink?"

"Well, I didn't really make it an option, but he didn't object. I guess if he wasn't going to get anything out of the evening, there was no point in being chivalrous."

Monique twisted her mouth into a cynical

knot, and Cara shook her head with disappointment.

"Still, I am so surprised," she told Monique. "He just seemed so nice and charming. I can't believe he would act that way."

Monique shrugged.

"I keep telling you, Cara, being single these days is a horrible experience. It is really hard to find normal, decent men. They all have some issues or character flaws. And any single guy would probably say the same about the women they are meeting. You are so lucky to have found Kyle when you did."

Both women looked over at the topic of her comment. He was still holding Meghan and feeding her small morsels from his plate while showing polite interest in whatever Jones and Melissa were talking about.

Cara smiled softly, obviously still madly in love with her husband.

Melissa called out to the two women a few moments later, and started another topic of conversation. The group stayed around the table for another forty-five minutes, talking and sipping coffee long after their meals were finished. They then helped Cara bring everything back inside and clean up the kitchen.

Monique had just finished loading the dishwasher when her cell phone rang. It took her a few rings to get it out of her purse, and she ended up missing the call. She didn't recognize the phone number. A couple of seconds later, the phone beeped to indicate that the caller had left a message. She was completely surprised by the voice that was recorded.

"Hey, Monique, it's Tao. Tao Samuels. I just wanted to make sure you are okay this morning. Anyway, give me a call when you have a second."

Monique replayed the message, mostly to hear his words again and assure herself that it wasn't her imagination. She then made sure to record his name in her phone and attach it to the cell phone number on the display.

"What's up?" Cara asked, noting the mixed look of surprise and pleasure on Monique's face. "Who called?"

"You're never going to believe this, Cara. Do you remember that guy on my basketball team I mentioned? Tao Samuels?"

"Hmm . . . the one who's mixed with something? Is it Japanese?"

"Chinese, actually. That's him. Well, I ran into him at the restaurant last night after Colin had left. We hung out a bit, then he offered to drive me home 'cause I was feeling a little tipsy," Monique explained, keeping her voice low like she was telling a secret. "So, we get to my house and he comes in so I can call him a cab. The next thing I know, we're all over each other! I mean kissing and making out really hot and heavy. I don't even remember how it got started."

"What happened?" prompted Cara, her dark, catlike eyes open wide with surprise.

"Nothing, that's it. We kissed for a bit then his ride came and he left."

"Are you sure? You did say you had been drinking."

"Yes, I was a little tipsy but I wasn't drunk. I remember almost everything except a few details," Monique explained with certainty. "Anyway, that was him calling. I didn't even know he had my cell phone number, but he must have gotten it from Gary."

"Well, what did he say?"

"Nothing really, just that he wanted to make sure I was okay this morning."

Both women looked at each other, thinking about things and trying to make sense of it.

Monique finally shrugged and put her phone back in her purse.

"So, what happens now?" Cara asked.

"I don't know. Nothing, I guess."

"What do you mean 'nothing'? He's obviously interested in you!"

"I don't know. Tao is one of those guys . . . you know . . . really good looking, charming, way too many women. I'm not sure that's what I need right now. Plus, we're kind of friends. It's a little weird."

"Well, it's too late for that now, you guys have made out. So, you'll have to come to terms with being friends one way or the other. And plenty of good relationships start out as friendships."

Monique sighed. She was feeling perplexed about the situation. It wasn't just this new development with Tao, it was also her ambiguity about what she wanted in her life right now in terms of a relationship. The idea of pursuing something serious and committed really scared her to death. She just did not have the emotional strength to do it again anytime soon. But, there was no denying that she was lonely and missing physical male contact.

Her thoughts briefly went back to the conversation with Gary and the guys the day before. She had been kidding about the idea of a friend with benefits, but after the kiss with Tao, the concept did not seem like such a joke.

Chapter 7

By the time Wednesday came again, Monique had decided to stop sweating things. She still did not know what she wanted right now but also realized that making a decision would not really change her situation. It seemed smarter to stop thinking about things too much and move on with life.

She and Cara had debated the issue a little bit more on Sunday. Cara's opinion was that Monique needed to understand her issues about relationships right now, particularly her avoidance of getting into one, and decide what she did want. Cara was a firm believer in self-realization. Monique agreed in principle, but just could not muster the energy to apply that sort of organized, proactive thinking to her own situation right now. So, they agreed to disagree.

Though she waited until later Sunday afternoon when she got back home, Monique did return Tao's call. He answered after the first ring.

"Hello?"

"Hey, Tao, it's Monique," she replied, hoping her tone sounded light and casual.

"Hey, Monique. How's it going?"

"I'm okay," she told him. "Thanks again for driving me home last night."

"No problem. How did you feel this morning?" he asked.

She could hear a little bit of teasing in his voice.

"I was fine, actually."

There was a slight pause. Monique was going to change the subject to something more neutral, maybe ask him how his day was going, but Tao spoke first.

"Listen, Monique. I hope I didn't make you uncomfortable by kissing you. I wasn't trying to take advantage of the situation or anything. It kind of just happened. But I knew you weren't yourself, so I'll understand if it's something you regret."

Monique could not think of one thing to say in response. She just could not believe that Tao would put things out there like that, without subtlety or delicacy.

"Well. . . . Tao, I . . ." That was all she could come up with.

"Don't get me wrong. I thoroughly enjoyed the kiss. It was really hot, and pretty hard to stop. I'm just saying that I know it wasn't the right time, and . . ."

"No, Tao, it's okay. Really!" she interrupted, suddenly afraid of what else he would say. "It's no big deal. I guess it's just one of those things that happens."

Monique tried to sound laid-back and flippant, not wanting him to think she was putting too much importance on the incident. Instead, she came across as dismissive, even to her own ears, and she cringed.

"I mean, it was fine . . ." she tried to explain further, in a more approachable tone.

"Anyway, I just wanted to make sure things were cool," Tao stated, speaking over her and probably not hearing her words.

"Okay."

"So I guess I'll see you on Wednesday," he continued.

"Yeah, sure. I'll be there."

She hung up the phone, feeling a little dazed and a lot like an idiot. Her only defense was that his frankness caught her completely off guard. Monique had expected that Tao would either pretend the kiss had never happened, or maybe just flirt with her a little to gauge her reaction. It reminded her that, though they had hung out occasionally over the past few months, there was a lot she did not know about him.

Now, as she got dressed in the changing room for their Wednesday game, she tried not to be nervous or anxious. Yes, he was extremely attractive and sexy, and yes, their kiss had been pretty hot, but she was a mature woman and recognized that it could just be a brief, meaningless connection between them. It would be a big mistake to make it into anything more than that. Monique may not be able to stop thinking about the feel of his lips on hers, or how hard his arms felt under her fingers, but that was as far as she was willing to let it go.

She walked into the gym a couple of minutes before the game was to start. Tao gave her a casual nod, as did Gary. Monique thought she sensed a moment of tension, but she just smiled back then silently joined the rest of the team in some warm-up shots. A few of the guys asked her how she felt after her fall the week before, and she assured them that everything was fine.

Once the game started, things went back to normal. The team they were playing was pretty good, and the Ravens were having an off night. In the end, the score was pretty close, with the Ravens coming from behind in the last couple of minutes to win by just three points.

Monique was dripping with sweat when it was over. She grabbed the bottom of her team jersey and used the edge to wipe off her forehead and neck. The act inadvertently revealed her naked midriff almost up to the edge of her sports bra. She was about to drop the fabric when she caught Tao looking over at her from the corner of his eyes. To everyone else, it appeared that he was paying attention to the conversation going on between the guys around him. But Monique could feel the heat of his gaze even from halfway across the gym. She continued to feel his eyes on her as she walked out of the room.

Gary fell in step beside her as they walked to the changing rooms.

"Do you have time for dinner?" he asked her.

"Where are you guys going?" she inquired before deciding.

"Jimmy and Patrick suggested that pub down the street, McKenzie's. They have a few Wednesday-night specials."

Jimmy Gleeson and Patrick Johnson were two other guys on their team, who often went out with them after the games. Jimmy was married, and it appeared that this was the only legitimate time he could get away from his wife. Patrick had a girlfriend, but she was a nurse who worked evenings.

"Hmm . . . I'm not sure," Monique replied, not really feeling the idea of pub food.

"Come on. Nigel's going to come too."

The way that Gary made the statement caused her to look at him suspiciously. Nigel Whitehorse also played with them and was one of their starters. He was a quiet, slender guy about the same height as Monique, with a dark complexion and a razor-sharp face.

"Okay . . ." she said, dragging out the word to make it clear she really didn't understand what he was implying.

"Come on, Monique. You know he's interested in you," Gary insisted, with a mischievous smile on his face. "He's just slowly working his way up to actually asking you out."

Monique was already shaking her head long before Gary finished his statement. There was no way anything could ever happen between her and Nigel. He was just not her type, and his shyness and height were items on the long list of why nots.

"Gary, you know that I have no interest in Nigel."

He laughed out loud, already knowing that was going to be her answer.

"Yeah, I know, but the poor guy has been silently pining for weeks and is working up the courage to put it out there. Just hear him out, and then turn him down gently."

"Are you serious? He's really going to say something to me? Can't you talk him out of it?" Monique demanded, cringing at the thought of having to deal with the situation.

"I tried, but he thinks I'm just giving him a hard time. Plus, there is always that chance that you will consider it. I can't take away a man's dream like that!"

Monique rolled her eyes at his antics. Gary laughed harder, enjoying making her uncomfortable. They had reached the changing rooms a couple of minutes earlier while they talked. Tao approached them at that moment.

"We're still going to McKenzie's, right?" he asked as he opened the door to the men's area.

His question was directed at Gary, but Monique felt his eyes brush over her for a couple of seconds.

"Yeah," responded Gary.

"You're coming too, right, Monique?" Tao asked her, this time looking her directly in the eyes.

She nodded, not completely aware of what she was agreeing to.

"Great!" announced Gary, laughing with evil pleasure at the drama he thought would be the result of his meddling.

Monique headed into the shower a few minutes later, feeling a little dazed and unsure of how or why she had said yes to Tao. She didn't have any other plans for the evening, but she wasn't looking forward to the whole Nigel thing. Part of her knew that Nigel liked her, but she figured that it would just go away once she did not encourage him. But, if he was ready to make a move, it was probably better for her to address it now and be honest with him.

Her mind drifted back to the discussion she had with Gary, Tao, and the other guys on Saturday. While she definitely was not looking for a relationship right now, the idea of having a casual companion and intimate partner sounded like a great idea. Monique had only been half-joking when she told the guys that it sounded like the perfect situation. Nigel might be the perfect guy for an arrangement like that. He was a nice, decent guy. It's just too bad that she did not feel one ounce of attraction to him.

Now, Tao was a different story. Monique had always thought he was extremely sexy. Those eyes, lips, and perfect body probably created indecent thoughts in almost every woman he met. She could easily visualize having him as a lover, particularly after the kiss they had shared. And there was no doubt that he would be very good.

Monique was showered and dressed in her work clothes within twenty minutes. When she went back in to the hall, Tao, Scott, Jimmy, Patrick, and Nigel were already there, and Scott was telling them about some game he had watched the night before. Gary came out of the men's changing room a few seconds later. The group walked out to the parking lot and separated to put their gym bags in their cars before regrouping near the street.

McKenzie's was an Irish pub a couple of blocks away. It was almost eight-thirty when they arrived, and though it was quite busy inside, there were a lot of people leaving from the after-work crowd. The seven of them were seated at a large booth within a few minutes.

"How is your shoulder doing?" Nigel asked Monique.

They were all perusing the menu and the other guys were debating whether to get a large pitcher of beer. Nigel somehow managed to be seated beside her on her right while Gary was directly on her left. Tao was across from her at the end of the bench beside Jimmy.

"I'm okay. It really looked worse than it was," she told him while still looking over the menu.

"I was concerned about you all week," he told her. "But you played really well tonight."

Monique smiled at the compliment and looked at him briefly, not wanting to encourage him but also not intending to be rude.

"Nah, we were all a little off tonight," she surmised. "I missed several threes. And there was that lay-up . . ." She shook her head, indicting there was no adequate explanation.

"I know what you mean. We're lucky we didn't get murdered," he added.

The waitress came by and took their orders. The guys requested two pitchers of draft beer, while Monique settled for a sweetened iced tea. Everyone looked at her with disgust and teased her about being a good girl. Only Tao stayed silent, but his eyes sparkled with humor and she felt as though they were sharing a private joke.

Though Nigel tried to strike up a private conversation again, Monique deliberately involved herself in the group discussion. Gary had announced that he had gone out to the movies with a new girl on Sunday and was telling everyone about her.

"So, here's the thing," he began, letting them know there was an interesting story coming. "She works with my sister and called because she needed some work done on her car. I wasn't available when she needed it, but we stayed in touch for a few weeks. The last few conversations got pretty steamy somehow."

"Steamy, like how?" Jimmy asked, immediately sitting up taller in his seat.

"What do you think, moron?" threw in Scott.

"I'm just saying, were you talking about what you like and stuff? Or actually having phone sex?"

The other guys and Monique looked at him with mixed expressions of concern and exasperation.

"Okay, Jimmy. You need to get laid sometime this year or you're going to need medical attention," continued Scott, dripping with sarcasm.

Jimmy made a dismissive sound and went back to drinking his beer in silence.

"So," continued Gary. "We're getting along great, having some fun, and she sounds really sexy over the phone. We decide to go to the movies and meet for the first time. I'm so excited, and of course I'm imagining what she looks like."

"You didn't ask for a picture?" Scott asked.

"Crazy, I know. But it didn't come up at first, then later it didn't seem relevant," Gary explained, clearly regretting it. "Anyway, so she arrives at the theater and walks directly toward me. I told her what I would be wearing so she knew who I was right away. But even while she is approaching me, I never saw her. Or, if I did, it never occurred to me that it was her."

"Was she ugly?" Jimmy asked.

Gary paused, his eyes squinting as he thought about the question.

"Not ugly . . . but not at all what I expected. Just average."

"So, what's the problem?" asked Nigel.

Monique looked at him speculatively for a second.

"I lost all interest in her right away," Gary confessed bluntly. "I was so excited to meet her based on the all the stuff we had talked about. But the minute I looked at her, it was gone."

"You should have gotten a picture," Scott lectured again.

"Hold on," interrupted Tao. "Were you attracted to what you guys talked about, or to what you imagined she would look like while you guys were talking?"

"I don't know. Both I guess. But, even her voice didn't seem as sexy in person," explained Gary.

"That's messed up," said Scott.

The group sat in silence, taking a drink while thinking about the problem. Monique looked around at the men and wondered if this group was representative of the general male population. Jimmy, Patrick, and Scott seemed to get Gary's dilemma right away, while Nigel seemed to dismiss it as no big deal.

Once again, like the discussion on Saturday, Monique looked at Tao to gauge his thinking. His eyes met hers, and though the look in them was deep and intense, they were unreadable.

Chapter 8

"So, what happened?" Monique finally asked. "Did you guys have a good time at the movies?"

"It was okay," Gary told them. "She was nice enough. But I'm just not interested anymore."

"That's harsh," Nigel added.

"Maybe. But, I can't help it."

Monique could not help the look of disgust that passed over her face.

"What?" demanded Gary, knowing that there was something on her mind.

She let out a deep breath before driving forward.

"I get that you didn't find her physically attractive. But you were already attracted to who she was, what she had to say. Isn't that more important? So, she isn't gorgeous. Would it be better if she was really hot, but completely incapable of communicating?"

"See, that's the difference between men and women right there," announced Jimmy, before Gary had a chance to respond. "Men are visual.

That's just the way we are built. I have to say that most men would rather look at a beautiful woman than talk to a smart one."

Patrick and Scott nodded in agreement, while Nigel looked uncomfortable with the conclusion. It wasn't clear if it was because he disagreed, or reluctantly acknowledged it as the truth.

Tao had been fairly silent until that point. He understood exactly where Gary was coming from and had been in a similar situation more than once. So he understood what Scott was trying to say, but he had a different perspective.

"It depends on what you want," he finally told the group. His deep, authoritative voice made them all look at him, waiting for additional insight. "Sure, we like to look at beautiful women, and if that's all you're looking for, it's pretty easy to find. But a passionate, sexual woman is something totally different, and that has nothing to do with looks. So, Gary, you just have to decide which you're looking for. A man is really lucky if he can find both, but it's rare."

The guys seemed to think deeply about Tao's assessment, nodding while drinking their beer. Gary rubbed at the top of his head, trying to figure out if he knew the answer. But Tao wasn't paying attention to any of them. He was looking at Monique. She was stirring her sweet tea with her straw, looking down at the glass. Tao knew right away that she felt his gaze and was avoiding meeting his eyes.

She had to know that he was speaking directly to her.

That kiss on Saturday night was stuck in his head. Tao had relived it many times since then, remembering the feel of her lips, the taste of her mouth, and the heat when his tongue brushed hers. Most of all, he remembered how she responded to his touch. Before the kiss, she had leaned forward with anticipation. During the exchange, her body had sought the heat of his by brushing her hips against his. Tao could feel the hard peaks of her bare nipples right through her clothes.

In his mind, it had gone beyond just a kiss to become something far more intimate and sensual. He definitely wanted more of her. Now, he just had to figure out how to make it happen.

"I don't know, man," said Gary, finally replying to Tao's statement about the difference between a beautiful and sensual woman. "I see what you're saying. I guess I can call her and continue our phone conversations. They were pretty good. I will just picture Halle Barry the whole time."

"Gary, you're a pig!" declared Monique with disgust.

"What? I'm just being honest," he replied. "Be honest, don't you know guys you like as a person but just are not attracted to? This is the same thing. I might sound shallow about it, but it's no different."

Tao watched Monique's eyes open wide for a second, then look down as though embarrassed and uncomfortable. He immediately looked at Nigel, who sat beside her and seemed oblivious to the undercurrents in the conversation.

All the guys on the team knew how Nigel felt about Monique. It was sort of an ongoing joke because it was so obvious that she was completely out of his league. Nigel was a nice guy, with average looks, and he was a pretty sharp dresser. But he was so even-tempered that he came across as very somber and conservative. Tao just could not imagine that he would be able to handle a woman like Monique.

It had taken a while for Tao to start to understand Monique. She was always friendly and down to earth with all the guys, but she revealed very little about herself. Most of what he knew about her now and of her past came from Gary. But Tao also read a lot in her eyes and in the way she played ball. On the court, she was an unselfish team player. She was also strong-willed, determined, and competitive, and Tao could tell that those traits probably carried over to her professional and personal life. It would take a certain type of man to manage it.

Then, there was the fire hidden behind her deep, smoky eyes. Their eyes had met more than once over the last few months, and Tao was certain she had felt the same spark he had. There was also the way her gaze would occasionally follow his actions or travel over his body. She clearly did it unconsciously, almost against her will. Tao was used to women looking at him, and he was smart enough to know it had more to do with his mixed heritage and athleticism than his personality. He knew the difference between a look and a come-on, but Monique had never given any indication that she was interested in anything between them. He had always found her attractive and appealing, but had left it alone.

But that kiss they shared confirmed for him that those sexy eyes really did reveal smoldering passion and sensuality. Now Tao was absolutely certain that Nigel could not handle Monique Evans.

Their food arrived a few minutes later, and the general conversation switched to other things. Tao participated a bit, but he was distracted watching Nigel attempt to engage Monique in some private discussion. She was polite, but also clearly trying to let him know she wasn't interested. Tao found it pretty funny and could not hide his amusement whenever she happened to look over at him.

The group stayed at McKenzie's until a few minutes to ten o'clock. Jimmy and Scott were the first to leave after throwing down some money to cover their part of the tab. Patrick left a few minutes later. Tao and Gary had come together and were still finishing their beers, but Nigel kept looking at his watch.

"Are you ready to go?" Nigel asked Monique. "I'll walk back with you."

"Hmm, I have to pick something up nearby," she told him. "You go ahead."

Nigel looked uncertain about what to do and opened his mouth, perhaps to offer to go with her. But Monique quickly pushed her chair back and announced that she needed to use the bathroom. The three men watched her leave.

Tao and Gary looked at each other, waiting to see if Nigel was going to mention his lack of success with Monique so far. It took him only about half a minute to bring it up.

"I was going to ask her out for this weekend. What do you think?"

The question was directed at Gary, so Tao used the opportunity to head to the bathroom as well. As he walked away, he heard Gary start to tell Nigel that it might not be a good idea. Tao knew that Gary would fill him in on the details later.

As he hoped, Monique was coming out of the women's bathroom just as he got to the back of the pub.

"Hey," he said as he stopped in front of her.

"Hey," she replied, clearly surprised to see him appear. "Is Nigel still here?"

"Yeah. You know you're going to have to be honest with him if you're not interested."

Tao said the words with quiet intensity, catching her gaze and holding it. She searched his eyes, almost hoping that he would reveal some other, easier alternative to blunt frankness.

"I know," she finally admitted. "Damn, I hate this. I don't want to hurt him, or have him feel weird about it after. There's nothing wrong with him. It's just there's no . . ."

"Sparks," he filled in for her. "Don't feel bad about it. It's either there or not. You will be doing him a favor to be clear about things up front. It will save him a lot of heartache in the end. Nigel's a good guy. He'll get over it."

"I guess," Monique replied, clearly miserable about having to deal with it at all.

Tao watched the emotions pass across her face and loved how her eyes revealed her turmoil.

"At the same time, if you're not feeling what I'm feeling between us, I want you to be honest with me."

Her eyes flew to his, clearly shocked that he would put things out there like that.

Tao had not planned to start a discussion about them at that moment. He had wanted to meet up with her before she came back to the table just to have a few moments alone. But the words came out of his mouth before he could hold them back. Now he wanted to hear her response. It took her a few moments to say anything and he enjoyed watching her discomfort as she formulated an answer. It never occurred to him that she would say she wasn't interested.

"You're kind of blunt, aren't you?" she told him, her focus somewhere over his shoulder.

"I can be."

Monique nodded, clearly still buying time to come up with a good answer.

"Well, I'm not sure what I'm feeling between us," she eventually told him.

A big smile spread across Tao's face, revealing his strong, white teeth.

"But there is something, right? It's pretty hard to ignore and I noticed it from the first time we met. Now I know our kiss was inevitable. I completely enjoyed it, and I want to do it again."

He spoke in a low, melodic voice, dripping with

intensity and suggestion. Monique was looking up at him, as if mesmerized by the words. Her lips were parted like she was waiting for him to show her what he wanted. Tao started to lean forward, wanting to taste the flavor of her mouth, completely forgetting where they were.

"There you guys are," said Gary from somewhere behind Tao.

Monique quickly stepped back, and Tao straightened up and turned to face their friend.

"Are you guys ready?" Gary asked, completely oblivious to the tension between them. "Nigel already left."

"Yeah," Tao told him. He was looking down at Monique, while she looked at Gary with a blank face.

"Okay, I'm just going to run to the bathroom" Gary explained as he walked around them and into the men's bathroom.

"Do you want to stay for a bit?" Tao asked her. "You can drop me at Gary's after. Don't worry; I'll give him a good excuse. Meet me at our table."

Tao didn't really wait for her to respond before he also went into the bathroom. Gary was washing his hands and Tao casually went to the urinal.

"I'm going to talk to Monique for a bit about how I can grow my business," he told Gary casually. "It sounds like she has some ideas, so we'll just hang out here for a bit and she can drive me home later."

Tao had mentioned to Gary a couple of times in the last few weeks that he was considering growing his security consulting business by bidding for larger contracts and hiring a couple of employees. Gary was actually the one who had suggested that Monique may be a good resource with her extensive background in sales.

"Okay, cool," Gary replied with a nod, completely unfazed. "I'll catch you later."

Chapter 9

Monique was surprised to find herself sitting back at their table, waiting for Tao. Their waitress was in the process of cleaning up and Monique asked for another glass of sweet tea. A few minutes later, Gary walked through the restaurant and out the front door, waving to Monique as he passed by. Then there were another couple of minutes where she sat alone, wondering how she had gotten into this situation.

She reviewed the last ten minutes in her mind and realized that Tao Samuels had completely taken charge of the situation and everyone else had just naturally fallen into line, including her. It had not appeared deliberate or manipulative, more like natural leadership to make things happen. Monique marveled at the effortless ability and wondered if it was a result of his military training, or just inherent to his personality. She also wondered why on earth she had gone along with his request, which bordered on an order. That was definitely out of character for her.

Tao got back to the table around the same time as the waitress was bringing her new drink. He used that moment to order a glass of draft beer.

"Do you always order people around like that?" she asked once he was seated.

"What do you mean?" he replied.

Monique could not tell if his confusion was genuine or feigned but assumed the latter for the sake of her argument.

"You know exactly what I mean. You ordered me to go and wait for you here, and didn't wait for a response."

"I didn't order you. I asked you. I figured that if you didn't want to, you would say no or just not go," he explained, apparently unfazed by her accusation. "Are you saying that you didn't want to stay and talk more? You could have refused. Or ducked me by saying you had to pick up something nearby."

Monique immediately recognized the sarcastic reference to her earlier comment to Nigel. She opened her mouth to shoot back a stinging answer, but nothing appropriate came to mind. His lips twisted in a cunning grin, as though he knew she was stumped. Monique fought the urge to punch him hard, preferably somewhere that would do some damage to his pretty face. She sucked her tongue with irritation instead.

"So we're here, alone, as we both wanted," he continued. "I think we should use the opportunity to be honest with each other."

There was that word again, Monique thought

to herself. Honesty. Everyone had a different interpretation of what it really meant to be honest, particularly in a personal relationship. For her, it meant vulnerability and exposure to pain and deception. She had been honest with Donald about her feelings for him and her willingness to wait for him to resolve his marriage situation. That honesty gave him the weapon he needed to use and manipulate her. Now Monique just wasn't sure she could be honest with a man like that ever again.

"Okay," she said to Tao, pulling herself together and taking a defensive stance. "Let's be honest. I won't deny that I find you very attractive, and I do feel something between us. But I'm not looking for a relationship right now. I don't really have the time or energy to put into one."

"Why not?" he asked simply.

Monique shrugged cavalierly. "It just doesn't appeal to me right now. I got out of a pretty intense one not too long ago, and I don't want to go there again."

"Right, the married guy," he replied, nodding with acknowledgment. "Okay. That's what you don't want. What do you want?"

"What do you mean?"

"You don't want a relationship. It's not the first time I've heard you say that. But what *do* you want? Friendship? Intimacy? Companionship? Those are all different from a committed relationship."

He had summed up all of the thoughts and options Monique had been struggling with over the last few weeks, and particularly since Saturday. She honestly did not have an answer.

"More specifically, what do you want from me?" he continued.

"I don't want anything from you, Tao," she immediately replied.

"Monique, we said we would be honest. I want to build on what happened on Saturday. I want to kiss you again, touch you while you're in my arms, see if we want to do more. I want to continue our friendship. Eventually, I do want a long-term relationship with someone, but that can wait until I know I've met the right person. What do you want from me?"

Once again, Monique found herself mesmerized and a little in shock at how easy it was for him to put his thoughts and feelings out there without any apparent fear of rejection. She wasn't sure she had ever met someone so at ease with expressing himself.

"I don't know," she finally told him.

"Come on, you can do better than that," Tao encouraged.

"Really? Are you just looking for an ego boost? What do you want me to say? That I want you to kiss me again? That I've thought about doing more? That I want you?"

She tried to sound biting and sarcastic, but Monique didn't quite pull it off.

"That's exactly what I want you to say, if it's true," replied Tao. "And it's not about me, or an ego boost. It's only about you. I want to understand you, and find out what can I do to satisfy you."

Monique suppressed her immediate urge to snap back, something she often did when she felt cornered. Tao's tone was completely patient and tolerant, as though he was coaching her on how to participate in his verbal intimacy.

She let out a deep breath and took a long sip from her cold drink. When she found the courage to look up at him again, it was to find him completely relaxed and waiting for her to speak again. There just didn't seem to be a reason not to put things out there.

"All right. I want to kiss you again."

Tao's expression did not change, but there seemed to be an electric charge that ignited between them.

"On a larger scale, I do want friendship and intimacy," she added.

He smiled briefly and sat forward so their faces were close together and he could talk in a quiet voice.

"So no companionship? Like dinners or the movies or romantic walks in the park? Just friendship and intimacy?" he questioned.

"You're teasing me," Monique stated, with a flash of annoyance.

"Maybe just a little," replied Tao, not at all intimidated by her sharp tongue. "But seriously, let's start with those two things and see what develops."

"Nothing will develop, Tao. I am serious. I don't want anything more and I'm not going to change my mind."

"Okay," he acknowledged. "So, we have the

friendship already. Let's develop the intimacy. What are you doing on Friday evening?"

Just like that? Monique thought, a little blown away by how quickly things had moved.

"Nothing," she replied.

"How about I come by your place? About seven o'clock?" Tao suggested. "I'll bring dinner. Do you like Thai food? There is a restaurant near my office that does great green curries."

Monique must have nodded, though she didn't remember doing so. Tao continued talking about things related to getting together on Friday. She listened, but later could not recall exactly what was said. They stayed at McKenzie's for another half hour until he finished his beer, then they walked to her car still parked in front of the gym. There were no intimate touches or contact. They could appear to be just two teammates walking together, but there was a new tension between them that was unmistakable and impossible to ignore.

While Monique drove him home, they continued to talk about a few casual topics. When they pulled into Gary's driveway, she stopped the car but did not shut off the engine.

"So, Friday at seven, right?" Tao said as he turned in his seat to face her.

Monique nodded, unable to formulate something more to say. Her thoughts were focused on whether he would kiss her again. She watched his mouth moving as he said something about her driving home safely. The full lips curled sensuously, showing a glimpse of beautiful teeth and a thick tongue. Would he taste and feel as good as she remembered? Should she lean forward and show him want she wanted?

She wasn't sure how long they sat in the idling car, but eventually the opportunity passed. Tao opened the passenger door and uncurled his long body to step outside. Monique felt an intense mix of disappointment and regret as she watched him walk away. It took her a few seconds to recover, then she drove home with her mind on everything but the road.

The sense of daze and disbelief stayed with her all day Thursday. Work started out extremely busy, with the sales team rushing to complete a proposal before noon. Once the package was printed off and in the hands of the courier, Monique rushed out of the office to meet Cara and her other friend, Tammy, for lunch at a small restaurant downtown. She arrived about twenty minutes late and found the girls seated on the patio. They had already ordered their meals and were chatting away.

"Sorry, guys," she stated as she slid into one of the free seats.

"No problem," Cara replied with a pleasant smile. "How did it go?"

Monique had spoken to Cara earlier, explaining that she might not be able to make it for lunch and why.

"Not bad in the end, but everything that could go wrong, did, of course! You know how it is; no matter how many people spellcheck it, there is always one mistake that no one sees until everything is printed," she told them, now able to laugh a little and release some lingering stress.

"I know!" agreed Tammy. She was a corporate lawyer in a large firm in the city. "It seems like those things never go smoothly no matter how much time you have and how much you prepare."

"Tell me about it," added Monique. "Okay, so what did I miss?"

"Well, Tammy was just starting to tell me about her first date with Alfred," Cara explained.

"Alfred? That's the fireman that you met online?" Monique questioned. "The one you've been flirting with?"

Tammy nodded.

"I was just saying that he checked into a hotel for the weekend. He lives somewhere north of LA so was supposed to be staying in San Diego for the weekend to visit with some friends. We met at a really expensive restaurant in Little Italy. He brought me flowers and a cute card."

"Are you serious?" Cara blurted out, cutting Tammy off. "He brought you flowers on the first date? Does anyone still do that?"

"I know!" replied Tammy. "I thought it was a little weird but, whatever, right? So we had dinner and he pays for everything. It was perfect. We laughed a lot, and he seemed so charming. We went for a walk for a bit, then he suggested we go to his hotel for a drink."

The girls looked at each other with grins, silently sharing their familiarity of where things were going.

"Tammy, you slut!" giggled Monique.

They all laughed, and Tammy covered her mouth to show a little shame.

"So, what happened?" urged Cara.

"Long story short, we ended up in his room."

Monique and Cara laughed harder.

"But, that's not the end of it! Okay, you have to picture this guy: six feet, three inches, and at least 230 pounds. A big, masculine firefighter with gorgeous blue eyes, a dark, copper tan, and jet-black hair. I mean, he is ten times better looking in person than those pictures I sent you guys. So, we're doing it, and it's pretty good. . . . Then, I swear on my life, guys, he has an orgasm, then goes into seizures for about fifteen minutes!"

There were a few seconds of silence as Monique and Cara looked at each other then back to Tammy with confusion.

"Wait, what do you mean?" Monique finally asked.

"I'm not kidding! He was moaning and shaking and convulsing for at least fifteen minutes! And whimpering like a baby! Guys, I was scared out of my mind! I tried to touch him, you know, ask him if he was okay, but he freaked out, screaming, 'Don't touch me, don't touch me. I'm too sensitive right now!'"

Tammy tried to imitate what her date would have sounded like in the throes of his bizarre episode. Monique and Cara burst out in shocked laughter. Tammy soon joined them until they were all laughing so hard that tears started to pour out of their eyes.

"I couldn't believe it! He was crying like a baby, shivering and everything."

"Tammy, I've never heard of anything like this before," Cara told her once she was calm enough to talk.

"I know! And all I kept thinking was that no one knew where I was. What if this psycho freaked out and did something to me?"

"So, what happened?" Monique finally asked.

"Well, he finally calmed down, and of course I asked him if it was always like that for him. He said sometimes but never that intense. And that was it. I got dressed and we talked about getting together again over the weekend. Then the asshole never called me!"

"You're kidding!" stated Cara.

"Unbelievable," chimed in Monique. "After all of that, he has the nerve to blow you off?"

"Well, maybe he's embarrassed, Tammy," Cara added. "I mean, it can't be easy for him to respond to sex that way."

"I don't know. But I have to tell you, I am so turned off by the whole dating scene," Tammy confessed. "The Alfred thing is just bizarre, but really, he's just like all the rest out there. I always seem to meet men who are either immature or just messed up!"

The other two women nodded with understanding. Cara was happily married and Monique had been out of the dating scene for several years, but both had other girlfriends feeling the same sense of frustration that they could easily relate.

"Well, I think women are trying to meet men in the wrong places. You have to move away from the clubs and parties. Those guys are just looking for a good time. Even if they meet the perfect woman, they wouldn't recognize her," Cara stated.

"That may be true, Cara, but I think women have a false image of relationships and love," Monique replied. "So, no matter how hard we look for it, we're not going to find it. Society sells us this idea that you will meet the perfect man: handsome, smart, and financially stable. We will fall in love, get married, then live this fabulous life. It just doesn't happen."

"It can," insisted Tammy. "Look at Cara, Monique. You can't deny that she found that man."

Cara was already shaking her head with denial.

"No, that's not my life at all, Tammy," she insisted. "I know it looks that way now, but when I met Kyle, he wasn't handsome, or financially stable. And we had lots of really tough times that weren't so good. Even now, I wonder if it's all worth it. I love him, I know that, but it's not what I thought love was. And I have to admit that I sometimes wonder if I've settled for what's comfortable. Having a little more money just makes it harder to know why you're with someone."

Cara spoke the words softly, almost as a whisper and as though she was telling a deep secret for the first time. Her friends looked at each other then back at her. She smiled at them, trying to lessen some of the tension floating around the table.

"So, maybe you're right, Monique. Maybe love is not what we're told it is, and it's time that women stop chasing a fantasy," Cara concluded.

Chapter 10

By the time Friday evening came around, Monique was in a state of apprehension and confusion. There were so many questions and doubts in her mind about how to handle the situation, and no one to talk to about it. Between Thursday and Friday, she had picked up the phone on at least three occasions to call Cara and spill her guts about this thing with Tao, but she'd chickened out and hung up. It also crossed her mind to talk to Gary, but again, she hesitated. They had been friends for years, and she had told him many personal things about her disastrous relationship with Donald. This was different, though. Tao was a good friend of Gary's and by confiding in Gary, she may cause friction between all of them.

The more Monique thought about developing something between Tao and herself, the more it was clear that there were many things that could go wrong. She even wondered if it was more trouble than it was worth, until she remembered Tao lips and the intense look in his exotic eyes.

Somewhere over her lunch break, she acknowledged that a strictly sexual relationship had too many benefits to ignore. There just needed to be a few clearly defined rules, that's all. She even took the initiative to write out three that she felt were essential.

By the time that seven o'clock rolled around that evening, Monique was feeling more in control. Tao had phoned her at around five-thirty on her cell phone to confirm their plans, but she had been on a conference call at the time so they had only spoken for a few seconds. She got home from work after six o'clock, with just enough time to shower and change into a pair of jeans and a fitted T-shirt.

Monique thought about making something for dinner, but then reminded herself that this was not a date, so cooking for Tao was inappropriate. She also remembered that he had promised to bring them some food.

She was in the process of opening a bottle of California white wine when the doorbell rang. Monique could not resist checking her appearance in a wall mirror in the front hall before she opened the door. Tao Samuels stood in front of her, looking more delicious than she could have imagined. He also had a large brown bag in his hands that looked like takeout food and smelled like something spicy.

"Hey, Monique," he said with a slight smile that only lifted the right corner of his lips.

"Hey," she replied, then stepped back so that he could come inside.

As he passed by her, she could smell the soft scent of bath soap and deodorant. She also noticed the way his blue cotton button-down shirt fit well across his broad shoulders, then fell over dark blue jeans that clung slightly to his thick thighs before falling loosely over his dark brown sneakers.

"I was going to get us some Thai food, but I haven't had Jamaican food in a while. So I brought that instead," he told her, stepping out of his shoes.

"Jamaican food?" Monique questioned, a little overwhelmed by his presence.

"Yeah. Jerk chicken and rice from a place near my office."

"Okay. I haven't had jerk chicken in so long. Not since I left Detroit."

"Really? This place is really good. It's been a while, but sometimes I'm there several times a week." He straightened up to his full height and looked down at her, his eyes intently fixed on hers. "Did I tell you that my mom is Jamaican?"

"Really? I thought she was Chinese?" stated Monique, clearly confused.

"She's Chinese Jamaican, actually. There's a pretty big population there," he explained. "Do you want to eat in the living room?"

He was standing so close that it took Monique several seconds to process his words and the slight change in topic. She blinked several times and Tao raised his eyebrows, silently probing for an answer.

"Uhhh, yeah. That's fine," she finally agreed. "Did you want something to drink?"

Monique led him further into the house and stopped near the entrance to the kitchen.

"What do you have?"

"Orange juice, bottled water, beer . . ."

"I'll have some water, thanks."

She turned into the kitchen and grabbed two bottles of water. When she got to the living room, she found him sitting on the couch, unpacking the two meals from the paper bag. She handed him his drink and he passed her one of the Styrofoam boxes and a plastic knife and fork wrapped in a disposable napkin.

There were a few minutes of silence while they settled in and began to eat their meals. At some point, Monique turned on the television and a rerun of a primetime cartoon played in the background. Eventually, when their food was done, they both sat back to finish their water.

"That was great, Tao. Thanks for bringing dinner," she finally stated.

Tao nodded with acknowledgment and turned to face her but said nothing in return. She took a deep breath.

"So, how is the new place coming along?" she continued, then watched as he took the final swig of his water before resting the empty bottle on the coffee table.

"Not bad," he told her. "I was there yesterday. It's supposed to be ready in about two weeks. But we'll see. That's what they said more than a month ago, so who knows at this point."

His tone was laced with sarcasm, but lacked

WHAT LIES BETWEEN LOVERS   101

any anger or frustration. Monique could not help smiling, and Tao grinned back.

"At this rate, I should be moved in by Christmas," he continued.

They both laughed again, but her smiled faded as she watched him push her coffee table away from the couch, then slide onto the floor to walk on his knees, stopping in front of her legs. Her teeth clenched as he used his hands to gently spread her thighs and crept forward until his abdomen lightly brushed against the crotch of her jeans.

"What are you doing?" she asked in a soft, breathless voice.

"Well, now that we've had the appetizer, I thought we could move on to the main course."

Tao reached forward to put one hand behind her head and pulled her close enough to kiss. He started out by gently sweeping his lips across hers, teasing her with soft, feathery brushes. Then, the tip of his tongue brushed across her bottom lip. Monique sucked in a deep shuddering breath before kissing him back. She ran her lips over the softness of his, tasting his flesh and sucking their full folds into her mouth. Tao moaned, clearly enjoying her reaction. The kiss deepened as they both took turns sweeping their tongues into each other's mouths, going back and forth like a game of tag.

"Okay, wait," Monique finally gasped, pulling back from the embrace.

"Wait for what?" he uttered, running his hot

hands over her thighs, causing her brain function to temporarily pause.

"We have to talk about this," she stated. "If we're going to do this, then we have to agree about what *it* is."

"I thought we already did that," Tao replied.

"I know, but there are a few rules that I think we need to establish."

His eyes flew open, indicating that he was finally listening to her.

"Rules," he repeated. "Such as . . . ?"

Monique let out a deep breath and searched her frazzled brain for the mental list she had been mulling over for the last two days.

"Well, I think it's important that we be clear about what we're doing. We're friends and teammates, so a misunderstanding could get really complicated."

"Okay, I understand that. What sort of rules are you thinking of?"

He was still resting between her thighs, but now in a relaxed kneeling position with his hands resting on her knees.

"First, we need to agree that this is a casual, convenient arrangement. We have to be clear with each other and end it if it stops being convenient."

"You mean, if either of us gets into a serious relationship with someone else?" Tao asked.

Monique shrugged.

"If *you* meet someone else," she clarified. "I'm not interested in a serious relationship."

Tao's brows furrowed and he pursed his lips,

clearly finding her answer puzzling. But Monique continued before he could add any comments.

"The second rule is that this must be exclusive. I mean sexually exclusive. I'm not interested in sleeping with someone who is sleeping with other people," she stated.

She looked at him with challenging eyes, fully prepared to have him balk at the requirement. His lips twisted into that devilish smile.

"Okay, so this is a casual, convenient, and exclusive arrangement," he summarized.

"That's right. We agree that we will have no other sexual partners for as long as we are doing this."

"What else?" he demanded.

Monique let out a deep breath, a little surprised at how easily he was responding to her rules.

"There should be no expectations around things like daily phone calls or romantic time together. We don't have to go out for dinner or to the movies."

Tao was now grinning outright. Monique wanted to smack him but kept her cool.

"Okay, no romance."

"I didn't say no romance," she corrected. "I said no expectations of romantic gestures. I'm talking about dating behavior. We're not trying to build anything closer than what we already have, so there should be no expectations to spend time getting to know each other."

"Why not? I think learning more about each other will make our intimacy even better," challenged Tao.

"No, it think it will just confuse things and someone could get hurt."

"Are you trying to prevent me from getting my heart broken, Monique?" he teased. The devilish grin was back.

"Hardly, I think your heart is just fine," she snapped back.

"Then it's your heart that you're worried about."

Monique snapped her eyes at him with frustration. His smile only got bigger.

"Do you agree or not?" she finally demanded.

"Casual and convenient. Exclusive. No romantic expectations," he summarized, showing grave sincerity that she knew was contrived.

"Exactly. Is there anything you want to add?"

"The only thing I want is what I requested originally. Honesty. I want there to be no lies between us about what we want and what we have. Do you agree?"

His words hung between them for long moments. Even before she answered, Monique knew it would be the hardest rule of all to follow, and the only one she was already prepared to break if necessary.

"Agreed."

Chapter 11

Tao could not believe what a disaster the evening had turned into.

It was just after one in the morning and he had been home from Monique's place for at least forty minutes. Other than the ten minutes he had used to take a quick shower, Tao had spent most of the time lying on the bed in Gary's spare room, brooding over what had gone wrong.

Was it all that talk about rules and defining what they were doing? Was it his performance anxiety or Monique's obvious nervousness? He could not pinpoint exactly what was to blame, but it really didn't matter. There was only ever one opportunity to make a good first impression, and he failed miserably.

He turned on the flimsy double bed, moving from his side onto his back, trying to find the right position that would allow him to fall asleep.

In Tao's mind, when he thought about being with Monique, it had been smooth and romantic, full of passion and climactic moments. And he had thought about it nonstop since the moment they had made plans on Wednesday evening. The details had been fuzzy, but the image of total sexual satisfaction was clear. He had floated around with a cocky certainty that he would bring her ultimate pleasure, then follow her into his own climax, all while maintaining complete masculine control and finesse. Afterward, she would look at him with dazed eyes, completely overwhelmed by his performance and obviously wanting more.

What a load of crock! Tao would have smiled if he wasn't already groaning with self-disgust.

Their lovemaking had started out well enough. Once Monique had agreed to his only rule of honesty, Tao had put his energy into recapturing the heat between them. He began kissing her again and eventually she relaxed and joined him. The sparks lit up almost immediately, and soon they were all wrapped up in the sweet taste and feel of their mouths intertwined.

Tao wanted to touch her everywhere. He knew that her skin would feel like smooth satin, and her soft scent was already surrounding his senses. But, he kept his hands innocently on the tops of her thighs, to keep himself in check and to allow Monique's passion to build slowly. Eventually, her moans became breathless, and her hands began to roam his back. Tao took her cue and started to explore her body.

They were still in her living room, with Monique sitting back on the couch and Tao kneeling between her legs. He ran his hands over the lean length of her legs, then up her torso, stopping to brush his thumbs over the spot just under her breasts. She sucked in a deep breath, and he could feel the pulse of her heart through the fabric of her T-shirt.

Tao pulled his mouth away from hers so that he could look into her eyes. They were deep, dark pools of heat, matching the intensity that he knew shone in his. He held her gaze while stroking his hands around her ribcage and up her back. Her hair tickled his fingers, and he played with the soft mass. Both their mouths were open as they tried to control their labored breathing.

Eventually, Monique's taut puckered nipples were begging him for attention. Tao swept his eyes over them, and watched with fascination as they swelled and tightened further. He almost groaned with the anticipation of how they would feel and taste in his mouth. His eyes locked with hers again as he finally swept his large hands over both breasts, scraping the tips with his palms. Monique's eyes closed and her head fell back as a soft groan escaped her lips.

Tao's memories of the details were a little unclear after that. There was something so intimate and primal about Monique's reaction to his touch that he lost hold of his usually unshakeable willpower. He remembered experiencing a rush of need so overwhelming that he lost the ability to control it.

His hands roamed her sweet curves as they filled his hands with surprising fullness. It wasn't enough. Her top came off, thrown somewhere in the room. Tao took a moment to enjoy the view of firm breasts barely hidden behind a sexy, lacy black bra, until that too was off and flung away. Finally, he feasted on her naked flesh with his eyes, hands, and mouth. Her moans urged him on, and she ran her hands ran over his head and back, occasionally scoring his flesh with her nails.

Tao remembered snippets of time, like her pulling up his shirt, of him unbuttoning it and throwing it off. Their pants soon followed, but he wasn't sure who did what. He knew that he tried to stop, or at least slow down and recapture a more sensual and tender approach, but her eyes were so intense and her kisses too hot for him to resist. He wanted her so badly that it was like an intoxication.

He had managed to take protection out of his pocket and slip it on. Tao would like to think that he also took a few minutes to prepare Monique for him, and make sure she was ready. But his next vivid memory was the feel of slipping into her tight sheath. Everything after that was less specific and more a nebulous recollection of erotic sensations and urgent desire.

It was incredible at the time. Like being swept up in an uncontrollable wave that was so overwhelming he could not care where or when he would land in the end. He just wanted to ride it for as long as possible. But the reality was that he probably did not last more than a few minutes.

Even now, Tao's stomach clenched with the thought of how incredible and mind-blowing his climax had been. He was hard and throbbing again just from the thought of how perfectly her body had received him and how sweet it felt to explode deep inside her. And there was the need to know when he could experience it all again.

But despite all of that, there was the shame of behaving like a horny teenager having sex for the first time!

Tao ran a hand over his mouth and held it there to muffle a curse that he wanted to shout out in frustration. He then shuffled from his back onto his side again, still trying to get a position that would allow him to finally fall asleep. Lying on his stomach was impossible because he was now rock hard from reliving those moments with Monique.

The whole thing, from the moment he started kissing her again to the point where he came like a wild bucking animal, moaning her name over and over again, probably lasted twenty minutes. And half of that had been the slow, sensual kisses they had started with. That had to be an embarrassingly short record for thirty-three-year-old men who were more than experienced enough to do better. It was particularly hard for Tao to swallow because he had always prided himself with the ability to satisfy his partner and put her needs and pleasure first. Yet that night, he had come across as unskilled and selfish.

Once the thunderous quivers of his climax ended, leaving him exhausted and sated, Tao found himself still on his knees between Monique's thighs. Her legs were draped over his shoulders and her soft round bottom pressed flush against his him. His now semisoft erection was still resting cozy and warm inside her.

Reality hit him pretty quickly at that point, and Tao remembered releasing his tight grip on her thighs and praying that he would not leave ugly bruises on her beautiful, flawless skin. Her eyes were closed, and her breathing deep and labored. They were both slick with sweat.

"Are you okay?" he finally asked.

Monique opened her eyes a little, then smiled softly.

"Umm, hmm," she said in tight voice.

It was clear that their position left her with limited air. Tao immediately lowered her legs so that she would be more comfortable. Their bodies finally separated, and the air around them felt cooler. Monique let out a deep breath and adjusted her position so that she was sitting up. She still had a lazy smile on her face, and it did a lot to improve Tao's self-respect.

"Wow," she said.

He leaned forward and pressed his lips on her forehead, then on the tip of her nose. She lifted her face so that they could share a soft, sweet kiss.

"That didn't quite turn out the way I had planned," Tao finally confessed.

To his surprise, Monique started laughing. It started out as a soft rumble in her chest, then progressed into a full belly laugh with her head thrown back. He really could not understand what tickled her so much, but she looked at his face and just laughed harder. His face must have shown a mix of shame and confusion because she finally calmed down a bit.

"Sorry," she finally gasped, putting a gentle hand on his cheek. Another giggle escaped her tightly clenched lips.

"You're laughing at me," Tao finally accused.

She shook her head, but kept her lips closed as though afraid more laughter would escape if she wasn't careful.

"So what's so funny, then?" he demanded.

"Nothing!" Monique finally denied. "It's just that I was thinking the same thing. This wasn't what I imagined it would be. We didn't even make it to the bedroom!"

She started to chuckle again, and Tao finally smirked, unable to deny the humor of the situation, particularly when he looked around at their clothes thrown everywhere, clearly discarded with desperate haste. His smirk turned into a toothy smile, though he still looked away from her eyes in shame. He pulled her close to wrap his thick arms around her and buried his face in the side of her neck.

"I didn't hurt you, did I?" he finally asked.

"No, I'm okay."

"Seriously, that was not what I intended. I wanted to go slow and focus on your pleasure."

"That's okay," replied Monique. "I think we both got a little caught up in the heat of the moment."

Tao could tell that she was making light of the situation if an effort to make him feel better. He wanted to say so many things to her; to tell her how much he had wanted her, how incredible she made him feel, how delicious it felt to be in her body, and that he had come so hard it made him feel dizzy. But, it was one of those rare moments in this life where he felt too awkward to be completely candid. Instead, he played it cool.

"It's still early. We have plenty of time to start over again," he told her.

Monique looked over his shoulder to check the time. Tao looked also and saw that it was only a quarter to ten.

"What do you have in mind?" asked Monique.

Tao didn't need any additional prompting. He stood up slowly, allowing his knees to unlock from their prolonged position, then extended a hand to her. Monique put her palm in his and let him pull her up until they were standing naked in front of each other. He took her by the back of the head and started a deep, sensual kiss that had them locked for several minutes.

"Let's go into the bedroom," he finally suggested.

Monique had that smoky look in her eyes again, then led him by his hand through the house until they were standing in front of her bed.

For the next hour, Tao did anything and everything that she could ever want. He caressed every inch of her flesh with his hand, worshiped every curve with his lips, bathed the secret folds with his tongue. He studied every moan and gasp she expressed to learn her body and discover her sweet spots. He made it his mission to bring her to the height of passion as many times as she could handle, and when Monique finally climaxed, Tao savored every scream from her lips and shudder of her body like a personal victory.

Afterward, they stayed lying in her bed for several minutes, not touching or talking. Eventually, she rolled off the bed and went to the bathroom. When the door closed behind her, Tao took it as his cue to get dressed. He was in the living room pulling on his shirt when she reappeared wearing a pair of cozy-looking cotton pajamas.

"Do you want some more water?" she asked as she headed into the kitchen.

"Yeah, sure."

That was the extent of the conversation between them. While he drank his water, she hovered near the foyer. Again, Tao took the hint and put down the half finished bottle on the kitchen counter. He casually walked to the front door and slipped on his shoes.

"I'll talk to you later," he finally said before he opened the door and stepped over the threshold.

Monique nodded.

Tao turned back at the last minute and kissed her gently on the lips.

"Have a good night sleep" he told her.

She seemed surprised, but nodded again. "You too," she finally responded, then closed the door behind him.

It was a long ride home for Tao, and now, sleep was eluding him.

He thrashed around for a bit and landed on his back again. Staring up at the ceiling, his mind wandered to the rules that he had carelessly agreed to earlier that night. *Casual and convenient. Exclusive. No romantic expectation. Honesty.* Unfortunately, Tao had already broken one rule and was rethinking at least two others.

Chapter 12

Thankfully, Tao did eventually fall asleep, but was up again at six-thirty on Saturday morning. It was a habit developed from more than thirteen years in the Navy. He thought about trying to get more sleep, but decided to go for a long run instead. When he got back, he took a long shower, then headed into the kitchen to make some coffee and have breakfast.

Gary sauntered in while Tao was pouring a bowl of cereal.

"Hey," mumbled Gary in a raspy voice.

"What's up?" Tao replied.

The two men were quiet while putting together their meals. They walked together into the living room to watch cartoons while they ate.

"How was last night?" he asked Gary.

Gary had announced yesterday that he was going on his second date with the phone sex girl, Luanne. Apparently, he was rethinking his view on the whole thing and trying to be more open-minded.

He shrugged and looked at Tao with a blank expression. Tao knew immediately that things had not gone very well.

"That bad, huh?"

"That's the thing," Gary explained. "It wasn't bad, just . . . okay. But, on the phone, before we met last week, there was this amazing chemistry and vibe going on. In person, nothing. We went for dinner, and we couldn't even think of anything to talk about."

"Wow, that's bad," added Tao.

"I don't get it. And she's not ugly or anything. But it's like I was attracted to the image I created and the real thing just ruined it."

"Well, that's the problem with Internet dating and long-distance relationships. You're getting to know the person in an artificial environment and there is way too much room for fantasy. Like you said, when you were on the phone with her, your imagination filled in the blanks. Then your attraction is not based on reality."

"Yeah, I know. It was dumb," Gary admitted.

"I saw it all the time while with military guys. They meet a girl just before a tour and spend the next six months or year e-mailing and sending letters. Next thing you know, they're convinced that they are in love. Some guys even proposed! And they'd probably only seen the girl two or three times," Tao explained while shaking his head. "Well, you can imagine how it ends. They eventually go home and find out that they didn't really know each other. It never works out."

"Well, that's the last time I'm going to do something like that," declared Gary.

"There's nothing wrong with starting a relationship over the phone or even the Internet. Sometimes that's just the way it works out. The problem is when people believe that they really know someone they've never met, or have met only a handful of times. There are some things that you can only tell about a person when you can look them in the eye."

"Like chemistry," Gary threw in.

"Exactly. Like chemistry. So, things with Luanne are definitely not going to happen, huh?" asked Tao.

"Nah, I don't think so. It's too bad. She seems like a nice lady."

"What wrong with nice?"

"Nothing! Honestly, if I had met her first and we became friends then maybe something could happen. She's not my type or anything, but you never know. But, on the phone, this girl had me so hot I was losing my mind! Now, when I look at her, I see my Mom's church friends and I can't even imagine kissing her!"

Tao could not help but burst out laughing. Gary made it sound so horrible that Luanne was a respectable girl and not a ghetto hoochie. The other guys were right, Gary really needed to reevaluate the type of women he dated. Jason and Isaac had included Tao in their criticism, but Tao knew it didn't apply to him. He usually knew exactly which category a woman fell into when he met her and wasn't confused about where she would fit into his life.

The two friends went back to watching cartoons, but Tao's thoughts wondered back to Mo-nique and their new arrangement.

She was an example of a woman with whom a man should not get involved unless he was thinking about a relationship. Monique was committed and serious about life in general, and definitely did not live for the moment. That was evident in her career and in her athletic ability. Tao had to admit it was those qualities that made her so attractive to him, along with stunning eyes and a sexy, lean body. Not to mention, there was an intangible spark between them that felt more like a strong electric current whenever they touched.

He could barely contain the cheesy smile that played on his lips whenever he thought about her. Even last night's fiasco made him grin with pleasure.

So the irony of the situation was not lost on him. Monique was definitely not the casual bed buddies–type of girl, yet that was what she claimed she wanted. He had not wanted to point it out to her yesterday, but the fact that she needed a list of rules under which to have a casual relationship meant that she was not cut out for casual relationships. Instead, Tao had decided to go along with her wishes. What was the harm? He figured that being with her under her terms was better than nothing at all. The rest would work itself out eventually.

The only question now was whether she was so

disgusted with his first performance that she wanted to cancel the whole thing. Tao could only hope that his encore presentation saved his reputation. Now that he'd had a taste of Monique Evans, there was no way he was going to walk away.

Tao hung out with Gary until about eleven-thirty that morning, then headed out to do some errands. His first stop was to pick up a few fixtures that he had ordered for the new apartment. It was a brand-new construction downtown. His unit was on the nineteenth floor with a stunning view over the San Diego Bay and the Pacific Ocean beyond that.

Though he had lived in Bakersfield, California, for most of his life, Tao spent many years in San Diego after joining the Navy. It became his second hometown, and it was an easy choice when he finally decided to retire and start his business providing corporate security solutions. His mom was disappointed that he was not moving back to her area, but she was used to his constant travel. Tao promised to return to Bakersfield often. Plus, his new place had two bedrooms, and he assured her that she could visit him regularly.

Tao's other errands included a stop at the barber shop for a cut, then a trip to the mall. His closet was a little thin on casual and work clothes. He wasn't a big fan of shopping, particularly in crowded shopping centers, but the situation could not be ignored anymore. Tao had a series of very important client meetings coming up in the next few weeks and he needed at least two new suits. He was a big guy at six feet, two inches, and 220 pounds, but he hoped there would be something suitable off the rack, maybe with a slight alteration.

Two hours later, Tao was in the car headed back to Gary's house. He had found a store with a large selection of clothes he liked, and he'd bought two suits in navy and gray, plus several shirts, ties, and a couple of pairs more of casual cotton twill pants.

It was almost five o'clock when he got home, and the house was empty. Tao expected that Gary would be home in the next little while. They were both going to a birthday party for a friend of Gary's, though Tao had also met her on a couple of occasions. They had agreed to leave the house at about seven o'clock.

Tao put his purchases in his room, then went into the kitchen and grabbed a bottle of water out of the fridge. He then headed out to the back of the house to sit on Gary's patio and relax for a few minutes, taking his cell phone with him.

He had been resisting the urge to call Monique all afternoon. Tao knew it was because of the rules that they had both agreed to. He didn't want to appear too anxious or demanding of her time, but at the same time, he wanted to see how she was doing and arrange to see her again. It was unlike him to be so unsure of himself, and it did not sit well with him.

Finally, he dialed her number. The phone rang four or five times, then went to her voice-mail. Tao left a very brief message just asking her to give him a call back when she was free. He then leaned back in the reclining lawn chair underneath the shade of a patio umbrella and promptly fell asleep.

When Gary finally woke him up, it was almost six-thirty. Tao then rushed to get in the shower and dressed for their friends' party. They left the house about one hour later, stopping at the liquor store along the way to buy two bottles of spirits to contribute to the bar.

Nicole Wentworth was the birthday girl, and she lived in a house with a couple of roommates in Mission Valley. When the guys arrived, the party was in full swing, with around fifty people already there. Most were standing around talking and holding various drinks. A few were dancing outside on the back patio.

"Happy birthday, Nicole," stated Gary, giving her a big hug. "You remember Tao, right?"

"Of course I do," she replied. "Hey, Tao."

Her eyes lit up as she looked up and down at Tao's tall, hard body, barely concealed in black slacks and a light blue golf shirt.

Tao nodded back while handing her the bottle of dark rum he had brought. He barely noticed her flirting. It wasn't that she was unattractive, far from it. Tao had noted her cute, curvy shape and pretty face the first time they had met. But tonight, he was preoccupied with wondering what Monique Evans was doing, when she would call him back, and if the music and talking inside the party was too loud for him to hear the cell phone ring.

Nicole led the guys farther into the house where they were welcomed by several people they knew. There were at least twice the number of women than men, and Gary noticed it right away, rubbing his hands together and giving Tao a look of pure delight. Tao had to admit that the women all looked pretty good, dressed to the nines in the latest casual styles. He politely smiled at a few who were particularly stunning.

"Now, this is my kind of party!" Gary declared as they continued through the crowd toward the kitchen and the food.

They were filling their plates with barbeque chicken, potato salad, and coleslaw when Gary looked out into the backyard to see who else was around.

"Hey, Monique is here," he declared.

Tao froze for a second, completely surprised by the statement. He then looked around, trying to see what Gary was talking about. Sure enough, he finally spotted her sitting in one of the plastic lawn chairs out on the patio. She was talking to a stunning woman wearing a sexy minidress. Her friend had skin the color of smooth dark chocolate, and a body built in a man's dreams: full and round in all the right places, trim and toned everywhere else. But Tao barely saw her. Monique filled his vision.

It had not occurred to him that she would be at Nicole's party, but now it seemed obvious that the two women would probably know each other through Gary. While Monique had met Gary while going to San Diego State, he had introduced her to many of his friends over the years, just as he had with Tao.

"Damn! Who is that girl she is with?" Gary asked.

"I don't know," replied Tao.

He appeared equally as transfixed as Tao was. They were both holding up the food line while they stared outside at the two women. A girl next to them cleared her throat, suggesting that she was tired of waiting for them to move out of the way. The guys took the hint and finished loading their plates, then Tao followed Gary outside.

"Hey, Monique," announced Gary as they approached the two women. "When did you get here?"

Monique stood up to give Gary a hug.

"About an hour ago," she replied. "Hey, Tao."

Her tone was very casual, but her eyes dark and elusive. Tao got the vibe that she expected him to act like there was nothing between them and was nervous about whether he would go along with it.

"What's up?" he replied, equally as laid-back.

Whatever silent communication that was being conveyed between them was interrupted by Gary's exaggerated clearing of his throat. Monique looked at him sharply, and he nudged his head toward her friend still sitting down. There was no subtlety there.

"Oh, my bad," stated Monique with dripping sarcasm. "Tammy, this is Gary Cooper and Tao Samuels. Gary, Tao, this is Tammy Wilcox."

"Nice to meet you, Tammy," Gary replied, turning on the charm. "So, how do you ladies know each other?"

Tammy smiled at the both of them while Monique took the opportunity to sit back down in her chair.

"I used to work with Monique at Sector Asset Solutions," she explained.

"Tammy is a corporate lawyer," Monique added. "She left the company back in the spring and now works for a big firm downtown."

Two people nearby suddenly got up to go back inside the house, freeing up a couple of chairs. Gary and Tao quickly claimed them, juggling their plates, and dragged the chairs over to where the girls were. Gary made of point of planting his seat next to Tammy's.

"A corporate lawyer," Gary repeated once they were settled. "That's pretty impressive."

"Not really," she replied. "It mostly about stacks and stacks of wordy contracts. Really boring, actually."

"Oh, I doubt that anything you do is boring," he countered.

Tao could only shake his head at his friend's lame line. But, surprisingly, Tammy giggled a little and raised a manicured hand to play with the buzzed back of her short, pixie hairstyle.

Monique, on the other hand, looked nauseated enough to throw up. She looked over at Tao, now sitting to her right, to share her disdain. He smiled back, and what should have been a quick glance turned into a long gaze filled with questions and unsaid words.

Chapter 13

Monique was the first to pull her eyes away. She could not believe how nervous she felt seeing Tao for the first time after last night. Thankfully, Gary had called her earlier in the day and told her that he and Tao would be here tonight, so she was mentally prepared for his arrival. But that did not stop her heart from beating and her stomach from clenching as he walked toward her.

He looked so delicious.

But he always looked good, particularly in loose gym shorts and a jersey that was wet with his sweat and sticking to every hard curve of his body. This was a different kind of good. His hair was freshly cut, low and sharp. He was wearing simple but stylish clothes, with a pair of well-polished black loafers. And he smelled wonderfully male, like fresh ginger, citrus, and amber. Monique felt like closing her eyes and leaning nearer to him, to fill her lungs with his scent.

Thankfully, the ongoing dialogue between

Gary and Tammy occasionally pulled her in, forcing her to stay focused.

"So, how do you guys know Monique?" she heard Tammy ask.

"We met in college," Gary told her. "I guess it's been about five years now, right, Monique?"

"Yeah, about that," she confirmed. "The same year that I moved to San Diego."

"I had seen her around the campus, hanging with some of the girls I knew. But then one day, a few of us guys were playing a game of three-on-three in the courtyard with these guys from another department. This one guy, Desmond, was our best player, but he had to run to class. So, we're about to forfeit the game, until Monique steps in and asks if she could play." Both Gary and Monique smile at the memory, while Tao and Tammy lean in to hear what happened. "Of course, we said no. I mean, we were playing rough and it was a bit of an ongoing grudge match with these guys. One thing was to forfeit, the other was to lose badly with a girl playing for us.

"Anyway, in the discussion, we pick up on Monique's accent, and once she said she was from Detroit, we started to look at things a little different, like maybe she had some streetball skills that we shouldn't turn down so quick."

"So what happened?" asked Tammy.

Tao had heard the story a couple of times, but it still amused him because it mimicked how he and the other guys felt when they considered her joining their men's league.

Gary chuckled and Monique looked down to hide her wicked grin.

"Let's just say you have never seen three guys so pissed in your life. The minute that Monique dropped the first three-pointer, they started cussing! But they had already agreed to the sub so there was nothing they could do without looking like sore losers. But we put a beat down on them that day. And it wasn't until after the game that she told us about her two NCAA national championships!"

Tammy looked at Monique with new eyes.

"Girl, I knew you liked to play basketball for fun, but you didn't tell me all that!"

Monique just shrugged. It was fun to hear Gary tell the story occasionally, but it seemed as though that part of her life was so long ago.

"So, these are the guys you play with now?" asked Tammy. "How come I've never been invited to a game?"

"Oh, please! You would be bored out of your mind, Tammy. I can't even get you to watch a game on TV." she snickered back.

"That's true," Tammy admitted, laughing good-naturedly. "But, this looks like it could be fun."

"Forget Monique. I'm inviting you to come out any time you want. We play pretty much every Wednesday at the gym in Balboa," Gary stated.

"I'll remember that," she told him, obviously flirting back.

For whatever reason, it had not occurred to Monique that Tammy and Gary would be interested in each other. Tammy had a habit of looking for men who had issues, and Gary seemed a little too normal for her. In the same way, she was a smart woman with a great career, the exact opposite of Gary's usual women. Yet Monique could feel the tension between them.

She looked away, trying to give the couple some privacy, and ended up locking eyes with Tao.

They smiled at each other, but Monique quickly looked away, unsure of what to say.

"Do you want anything to drink?" he finally asked her.

She had been sipping on a glass of white wine and still had half left.

"No, I'm good, thanks."

He nodded, then extended the offer to Tammy and Gary before heading into the house to get himself something. His chair was only empty for a minute or so before a guy name Albert sat down in it. Monique had met Albert before through Nicole and Gary, and knew that he was a bit loud and obnoxious. She was about to tell him that the seat was taken, but he immediately started talking and Monique could not get a word in.

By the time Tao came back, Albert was in the middle of one of his rants about something silly. Unfortunately, several of the guys around them outside found it amusing and kept encouraging his behavior, while everyone else tolerated him politely.

Tao handed a beer to Gary, then took a spot standing somewhere behind Monique's chair.

He didn't say anything, but she could feel his eyes burning the spot between her shoulder blades. Monique sat there for as long as she could without telling Albert to shut the hell up, or just taking him out with a sharp elbow to the nose. Finally, feeling confident that Gary would take care of Tammy, she stood up and told them both she had to go to bathroom. As she walked away, Monique could not help but glance toward Tao. Their eyes locked sending clear, silent communication.

He was right behind her when she reached the bathroom door.

"Do you always use the bathroom to arrange your rendezvous?"

Tao asked the question while stepping into the small room with her and closing the door behind them. They left the lights off. He whispered the words into the spot just above her ear.

"Rendezvous? That's a pretty military word. Are you suggesting that I wanted you to follow me?" she replied.

"You knew I would follow you."

She heard him press the lock on the door before wrapping his arms around her waist and pulling her up against him.

"I left you a message earlier," he added.

It was almost pitch black in there, but Monique closed her eyes while his lips brushed the side of her throat. She clenched her teeth when his tongue licked the tendon of her neck.

"I know, but I knew you were going to be here tonight."

"Is that why you wore this sexy dress? Is it for me?"

His hands brushed down her stomach, stopping at the top of her thighs. He bit her neck again. This time, she could not contain the excited gasp that escaped her lips.

"You look incredible tonight," continued Tao. "This is all I could think about from the moment I saw you."

"Really? So, last night wasn't enough for you?" she asked breathlessly.

"Not nearly enough. That was just the beginning."

Monique was excited and shocked when she felt him pull her dress up to her waist. His warms hand then slid over her thighs, first down the front then up her hamstrings and resting on her bum. He squeezed the firm flesh, then his fingers began to explore the texture of her soft bare skin.

"You're wearing a thong," he groaned softly.

"Tao . . . Tao, we can't do this here," she protested even as she bent forward slightly.

"I know," he replied, then slid one hand down the waistband of her panties. "I know."

One of his fingers slid along the ridges of her mound, then slipped into the center, now slick with her arousal.

"Tao . . ." She couldn't ask him to stop because she didn't want him to.

"I know," he repeated, his voice muffled into her neck. "But you feel so sweet."

His finger delved deeper until he pressed her button. Monique felt her knees buckle. She put her hands forward blindly until she found the wall. Tao circled the magic spot over and over again. Something about the dark little room, his cologne, the feel of his lips on her neck, and the party going on outside the door made her senses sharp and intense. She wanted to scream and moan, but bit her lower lip instead.

Then, Tao slipped the tip of his finger into her well. Monique groaned, and it sounded so loud in the room. He pressed in a little further and her breath started to come in little pants.

"Let's not stay at the party too long, okay?" he whispered. "I'll meet you back at your place after."

Monique could not understand how he could talk so clearly and rationally while she was losing her grip on reality.

"Uh, huh . . ." she managed to reply.

Tao stayed with her for another few seconds, then his hand was back on her hip, slipping her dress back into place. He pressed a lingering kiss just below her ear.

"Okay," he added. "I'll see you outside."

She heard the water run from the tap for a moment, then he was gone, closing the door again behind him.

It was a while before she could straighten up and turn on the lights. Her body felt like it was charged with electricity. When she looked in the mirror above the sink, her skin appeared flushed and her lips looked swollen. Monique wondered if everyone would immediately be able to see how stimulated she was the minute she went back outside.

She took a tissue and dabbed at her face to remove some of the shine. After a few moments, she gave up and let out a deep breath.

Suddenly, this arrangement with Tao Samuels did not seem very convenient! Monique had not planned for him to be able to make her hot and tongue-tied with just a look. Nor had she expected illicit encounters in public places. A casual, intimate relationship should be unemotional and controlled. The occasional encounter that was scheduled and satisfying until the need for sex revived itself. It was not supposed to be intense and overwhelming, leaving her panting for more.

That's how it had been last night. They had both been caught up in the moment, completely overwhelmed by this thing between them. Even today, Monique had trouble remembering all the details, other than the look of absolute abandon on Tao's face and the feel of his deep strokes at her core.

She let out another shaky breath.

This was not convenient at all!

Chapter 14

"Okay, what's going on between you and Tao Samuels?"

Monique and Tammy were standing in the corner of the kitchen, alone for the first time in a couple of hours. The partiers had just sung Happy Birthday to Nicole, and now they were all waiting around for a piece of cake.

"What are you talking about?" Monique asked.

"Oh, please, Monique," spat Tammy. "Anyone with eyes can see that you two are hot for each other."

Monique looked away.

"What's the big deal? He's not married, is he?"

She looked back at Tammy with hard eyes.

"Okay!" Tammy stated, taking a step back defensively. "He's not married. Sorry, I didn't mean to go there."

Monique looked away again.

"Seriously, Monique. Why the secrecy? So what if you guys have something going on?"

"It's a little complicated, that's all," she finally told Tammy.

"Why?"

While she wanted to keep things discreet, Monique could really use someone to talk to about things. And it seemed pretty silly to deny something that she was obviously not very good at hiding.

"Okay," she finally admitted. "Tao and I are . . . seeing each other. But, it's nothing serious. We're just being casual about things."

Tammy looked at her intently, silently asking a bunch of questions. Monique did not elaborate further, and the light finally turned on in her friend's head.

"Ahhh . . . It's like that! Well, I can't fault your taste, that's for sure," stated Tammy. "Just be careful, okay?"

"Trust me, I'm being careful. I was the one who insisted that it can't be serious between us. I am definitely not interested in falling in love and getting hurt again."

"The two things aren't automatically linked, you know? Being in love doesn't mean you will get hurt."

Monique's look at Tammy clearly said she was only tolerating Tammy's counseling, but she wasn't really listening.

"And you can't decide not to fall in love, Monique. It just happens."

Stubborn silence was the only response.

"Okay. You and Tao are friends, right? Which means that you like him. He's a good guy. Add great sex and his sexy looks. . . . Why wouldn't you want something serious with him? It sounds like the perfect relationship to me."

"Tammy, it is what it is. Don't make a big deal about it. This works for him and me for now. If it stops working, then we end it and stay friends."

"Well, since you have it all figured out . . ."

"That's right, it's all good. I know what I'm doing."

The words sounded familiar to both of them. Tammy didn't look at her, but Monique could sense what she was thinking. Those were the same words that Monique had used near the end of her relationship with Donald, when she still stubbornly insisted that he was about to get his divorce.

Though she and Tammy had known each other for about two years, they had not become closer friends until sometime in the spring of this year, just before Tammy had left the company for her new job. They started talking a bit, sharing personal information, and in one of those discussions, Monique had confessed her affair with a married man. Tammy had expressed her concern, but Monique had insisted that she knew what she was doing. Soon after, the reality of his betrayal became too obvious to ignore and she had finally ended the disastrous relationship.

Of course, since Donald had been a client of Sector Asset, she was very careful to be discreet and never mentioned his name to anyone at work, including Tammy.

Both women let the subject drop. It was almost

eleven-thirty and many of the guests were getting ready to leave the party. Monique knew that Gary and Tao were outside in the backyard somewhere. She and Tammy made their way out there to say good-bye. The guys were standing in the outer edge of a group of other men, and it was no surprise that Albert was in the center, carrying on loudly about something juvenile.

"Hey," Gary said as he saw them approach. His eyes brushed over Monique and settled on Tammy.

"We're about to get going," Monique stated. She looked at both Gary and Tao, trying not to behave conspicuously.

"Yeah, we're leaving soon too," Gary replied. "It was very nice meeting you, Tammy. You guys drive home safely."

"You too, Gary," Tammy replied with a flirty smile. "Bye, Tao."

"Bye, Tammy. See you later, Monique."

Monique's body had cooled considerably since the encounter in the bathroom, but Tao's words, said in such an innocent context, brought back a rush of excitement. She smiled casually before turning to leave with Tammy right behind her.

Tammy lived just north of the city and had picked up Monique to drive them to the party. The ride back to Monique's house was spent talking about Gary.

"So, you two seemed to have hit it off," Monique commented.

Tammy shrugged but had a pleased smile on her face.

"He seems like a good guy. Cute, too. He has really nice lips," she replied with a sparkle in her eyes. "But not really my type, though."

"I didn't think he was either. It never even occurred to me to hook you guys up, and it's weird that you haven't met until now. But, if you're looking for a good guy, you can't do much better than Gary. He's a mechanical engineer, very stable, and has always been a good friend."

"I can tell. But he just seems so . . . nice. I know, I know!" Tammy insisted before Monique could respond. "It sounds ridiculous. But, I can't help what I'm attracted to. I like men who are a little rough around the edges."

"Hey, I'm the last person to criticize anyone's decision when it comes to relationships," replied Monique. "But, if you are ready to step outside of your comfort zone a bit, Gary is a good choice."

"Did you guys ever have anything romantic?"

"Gary and I? No. We have always been like brothers and sisters."

Tammy nodded in understanding.

"Well, he seemed really interested in you, Tammy. So, what should I tell him if he wants your number?" Monique asked.

"He already gave me his. He told me to give him a call and maybe we could go out sometime."

"Really? Wow, he moves fast!"

Tammy shrugged again.

"He may not be exactly what I typically look for in a guy, but I'm single and available. It would be stupid for me to turn down a date with a nice

guy. I don't think there will be any sparks or anything, but at least we can have a nice time. What
do I have to lose, right?"

"That make sense," Monique concurred.

They talked a little more about dating in
general. It was a regular topic for them since
Tammy's dating fiascos have been a constant
source of amusement and dismay for them over
the last few months. No one who knew her could
understand how someone so sexy and smart could
continually meet all of the losers in San Diego.
Clearly, her choice of men was the problem, but
until Tammy was ready to look in another direction, Monique vowed to be supportive through her
struggles.

Monique was home a few minutes after midnight. She had invited Tammy in for a coffee, but
Tammy decided to drive straight home instead.
Unsure of how long it would take Tao to get to
her place, Monique went into her bedroom and
slipped out of her dress and into something
more comfortable. As she stood in front of her
closet wearing just her underwear, Monique
could not decide what to put on.

While dating Donald, they had a routine. They
usually got together in the early evening during
the week. Monique would rush home from work
to change into a sexy outfit, usually something
she had bought from an expensive lingerie store
or been given as a gift from Donald, a gift that
he expected to see her in. Her wardrobe now included a considerable number of see-through
babydolls, teddies, and novelty items trimmed

in feathers and fur. They had seemed fun and romantic at the time, but now she saw them for what they were: props in an elaborate game of lies that Monique had not known she was playing.

It was time to clear out her closet and throw everything to do with Donald in the trash, and she vowed to do it as soon as possible.

She pulled on a pair of black yoga shorts and a tank top, then went into the kitchen to get some water. Tao rang the doorbell about twenty minutes later while Monique was sitting in the living room flipping through the late-night channels on the television. She was suddenly hit with a bout of shyness and spent a few moments checking her reflection in the mirror next to the door.

Her intention was to act cool, invite him in, then slowly let things take their course. But Tao clearly had other intentions. Monique did not even get a chance to say hello before he pulled her into his arms and began kissing her intensely. It took her a few seconds before she could respond, and when she did, it was with equal fervor. His arms were wrapped around her back.

"I've been wanting to do that all night," he whispered, once they had come up for air. "Meeting you in the bathroom didn't help. You looked so good tonight."

Monique smiled shyly.

"Maybe we should get out of the doorway. I don't need my neighbors to see everything," she teased.

Tao laughed, then used his foot to close the front door.

"Good point," he replied. "Would you mind if I take you straight to your bedroom?"

Monique looked into his eyes and didn't need to respond. She took his hand and led the way.

Chapter 15

"Take off your clothes."

Tao was sitting on the edge of her bed and had already removed his shirt. Monique had stopped a couple of steps away to watch him reveal his incredible body, which was enhanced by the moonlight shining through her window. He gave the instructions just as he undid the waistband of his trousers and slid the zipper down. She was finding it hard to decipher his words.

Monique released a breath that had been held in anticipation. He lifted his hips slightly and slid the pants down his legs, kicking them aside when they reached his feet. Tao sat back down; he was wearing only boxer briefs, which clung to his hips and did little to hide the length of his erection.

"I want to see you naked," he added.

She felt mesmerized by the tone of his voice and the heat of his eyes on her body. Monique slowly removed her clothes, hesitating once she was down to her panties. She suddenly felt vulnerable and bare standing in front of him, with his eyes devouring every inch of her.

"Come here," he instructed.

She stepped into the space between his legs, a breath away but not actually touching. His eyes were directly in line with her naked breasts, enlarged in arousal and taut with anticipation. He reached out to pull her closer, his firm hands grasping her round bottom. Monique watched with fascination as he rubbed his full lips over her nipples. She waited as patiently as possible for him to take them into his mouth, maybe bite them gently. But Tao just took his time savoring the sensitive tips until she could not be patient anymore.

"Tao," she gasped in a voice that sounded hungry and urgent.

He looked up at her, and scraped his tongue over her hot flesh.

"Tell me what you want," he instructed.

Monique closed her eyes, wishing he would stop torturing her, but loving every aching second.

"Tell me," he demanded again.

"Ummm . . . I want . . . I want you to bite me,"

Finally, he opened his mouth and ran his row of even white teeth over her nipple. Monique moaned loudly in the darkened room.

"Is that what you wanted?" he asked.

He scraped his teeth over her bud again.

"Like that?"

"Yes, yes . . . suck on it . . ."

Tao did as she begged, using his tongue and mouth to pamper each breast with his attention while his hand continued to caress and mold the cheeks of her bottom. Monique felt as though every nerve in her body was singing. Her knees felt weak and she could not stop the shudders that ran up her spine. She was so lost in sensation that she barely noticed that he had slid off her panties until his fingers brushed over the dust of hair between her thighs.

"Oh, god," she muttered.

Tao delved deeper to stroke between her lower lips. She began to pant. He slid his long, middle finger slowly into her wetness.

"Hmm," he breathed. "You feel like silk."

Monique was beyond words. Her mind disappeared to a world where she could feel only his fingers and mouth. With her eyes closed and head flung back, she left her body in his hands to guide her on the journey to fulfillment. Tao took the reins and seemed to know exactly what to do. His sucking and biting became rhythmic and hot while his finger plunged strong and deep.

Her climax came fast and hard.

"Tao, Tao, Tao . . ." she chanted with each wave the crashed over her body.

It took several long minutes before Monique felt capable of rational thought and language skills. Tao had her captured in the curve of his arms while his hands caressed her back in long, soothing strokes. He pressed tender kisses along the tops of her breasts, occasionally pressing his check into the valley between them.

"That was incredible," he whispered. "You were incredible."

Monique giggled.

"No, *you* were incredible!" she insisted.

Tao tilted back his head and looked up at her.

"So, have I made up for my unimpressive performance yesterday?"

"What are you talking about?" she asked absently. "I thought yesterday was pretty good. Both times."

They both laughed.

Tao used the playful moment to pull her down onto the bed, then stretch out beside her so they were facing each other, lying on their sides.

"Well, I'm glad you enjoyed it. Even though it started out a little rushed," he told her.

Monique traced one of her fingers along his collarbone, then the solid slab of his chest.

"What I really enjoyed was seeing the mighty Tao Samuels lose his cool."

He didn't look away from her, but his expression was a mix of amusement and discomfort. Finally, he kissed her, softly at first, then with increasing urgency and fervor. Within minutes, they were both clinging to each other, breathing heavy with arousal. Tao rolled her onto her back, and Monique eagerly wrapped her powerful legs around his waist. He slid his straining arousal into her, burying himself to the hilt.

"Yes," he whispered while his lips were pressed into the crook of her neck. "Oh, yes, baby."

He withdrew from her warmth almost completely, then penetrated deep again.

"Oh, god," muttered Monique.

Tao laced his fingers through hers and started

a series of slow, torturous strokes. She could feel every inch of his hard length through every breath. Their bodies became slick with sweat and their whimpers and moans got louder and louder. His breathing changed to short pants and the grip on her hands tightened considerably. Monique felt her body mount to the crest of orgasm with him, and they went over the edge together.

They lay wrapped in each other's arms as the heat from their bodies cooled. When Monique finally stirred to throw her blanket over them, she wondered if they had fallen asleep for a period of time. Tao pulled her closer and helped to snuggle them under the covers. His eyes were still closed, but his fingers began to trace circles on her upper arm.

"Gary would not stop talking about Tammy the whole way home," he stated in a lazy voice.

"Really? It's weird. She's just not his type. He isn't hers either, for that matter. It is odd that they have never met, but I wouldn't have set them up anyway. I generally try to avoid match-making. It rarely turns out well," Monique explained.

She didn't hear his laughter, but felt the rumble in his chest.

"So, you're not going around pairing up all your single friends?" he teased.

"Definitely not! They are very capable of getting themselves into trouble all by themselves."

"Did you tell Tammy about us?"

The question caught her by surprise, and Monique took a couple of seconds to answer.

"No, but she eventually guessed. Apparently, you're not as discreet as you think."

"I wasn't trying to be discreet."

"So, you told Gary?" she asked, opening her eyes to look at him.

"No," Tao replied.

Monique closed her eyes again and returned to her relaxed position.

"I don't care if he knows, but I assumed you would prefer he didn't," he continued to explain. "It wasn't one of your rules, but I kind of got the sense you would rather keep this on the down-low."

"There really isn't any reason for him, or anyone else, to know, right?" insisted Monique. "It would just make things complicated, especially on the team. And, that would be against the rules."

"Yeah, but now Tammy knows. And from the way Gary took a shine to her, they might be spending a lot of time together."

"She won't say anything," she stated firmly.

"You seem pretty sure of that."

"I am. I don't have friends whom I don't trust."

"You're friends with Gary, but you don't trust him enough to tell him about us?" challenged Tao.

"That's different. It's not that I don't trust him. I just don't want to put him in an awkward situation, that's all. You and Tammy could easily never see each other again, so there is no harm in her knowing things."

His silence suggested he understood her point.

"Do you have a lot of friends in San Diego?" he finally asked.

Monique rolled into a more comfortable position on her side. Tao followed and spooned her from behind. She could not resist snuggling closer to his heat.

"Not too many here. Tammy and I have become pretty tight recently, then there is my best friend, Cara. We grew up together in Detroit, and her family moved here while we were in high school. She's the main reason I chose to move here."

"What about in Detroit? Lot's of family and friends?"

"A few. My mom and dad are still there, and I have two older brothers."

"Basketball players?" he asked.

Monique smiled. "Yeah! How did you know?" This time, she heard the rumble of his laughter.

"There is no way that you got those ball skills from some high school coach," insisted Tao.

They both laughed for a few seconds. He pulled her closer and she let him. Then they fell asleep.

Monique had a queen-size bed and was not used to sleeping with someone else. She liked to spread out in the middle of the mattress and roll around as needed for comfort. The sheets were usually a mess in the morning. That is why she woke up on Sunday feeling oddly restricted and a little disoriented.

Her eyes were still closed, but she could see the sunlight in the room as it filtered through her eyelids. She tried to roll from the position on her stomach, but couldn't. There seemed to be a weight pressing on her back, trapping her in place. Monique pushed up again a little harder and the weight moved a little. Then it made a grumbling sound and breathed out on her shoulder.

Her eyes flew open and everything came sharply into focus.

Tao was still asleep beside her, still cuddled. And from that raw heat emanating from his body, he was as naked as she was. Sensing her consciousness, he stirred a bit more and ran his hand over her back to rest on her bum.

"Good morning," he mumbled while pulling her closer to him. Monique immediately felt the nudge of his morning erection.

"Morning," she replied.

"What time is it?"

"I don't know," Monique admitted, then shifted around until she could see her alarm clock on the night table beside her. "Quarter to nine."

"Hmm. That late? I never sleep in," replied Tao, clearly surprised.

Monique didn't respond. She wasn't sure what to say. This wasn't part of her plan. The casual relationship she wanted did not include sleeping in one another's arms or cuddling in the morning. It definitely did not include morning sex. That was a couple thing, and completely inappropriate. Somewhere in the back of her mind, she had expected Tao to get dressed and leave her house sometime in the middle of the night. That's what Donald always did. Monique was used to waking up alone the morning after, and she had not intended to change that.

Clearly, Tao Samuels had other ideas as he continued to caress her skin. The hot brand of his arousal seemed to poke her hip even harder.

"Did you sleep okay?" he asked.

"Hmm," she replied vaguely.

She was too busy trying to figure out how to handle the situation and could not take a second to assess how well rested she felt.

"I slept like a log!" Tao added. "Honestly, I don't even remember falling asleep. I remember everything before that, though."

There was a teasing tone in his voice, but Monique didn't respond to it. A few seconds ticked by and she remained stiff and detached. She knew the minute he sensed her mood, because his fingers stopped roaming over her skin.

"Are you okay?" he finally asked

"Ummm, yeah. I'm okay," she replied hesitantly. "It's just that I'm not used to sleeping with anyone. I'm actually really surprised that I was able to sleep with you still here at all. I guess I expected that you would leave. . . . You know . . . when we were finished."

Tao didn't respond right away, nor did he move.

"Okay," he finally said, dragging out the word, clearly expressing that he didn't really understand what she was saying. "I'm surprised I fell asleep so quickly. But, did you want me to sneak out in the dark, without waking you up?"

When he put it like that, it did sound a bit cheap and silly.

"No! Of course not!" she insisted. "It's just weird for me, that's all."

"Would you rather I leave?"

Monique took a moment too long to answer. Tao took the hint and rolled away from her. When she sat up and looked around, he was sitting on the edge of the bed.

"You don't have to leave," she stated finally.

"I think I should."

His words were simple and void of any emotion. Monique immediately felt like an idiot. She watched him stand up then start to search around for his clothes.

"Seriously, Tao. You don't have to rush off. Why don't I at least make us some coffee."

"Don't worry about it, it's no big deal," he replied. "I'll just use your bathroom then I'll get going. I had some things planned this morning anyway."

The silence stretched awkwardly between them as he pulled on his clothes then walked into her en suite bathroom and closed the door behind him. Monique felt dejected. It was clear that she had blown the whole thing out of proportion and now there was this awkwardness between them. Now that he was about to leave, she had to admit it would have been nice to spend some more time together, maybe have breakfast and go for a walk on the beach.

Tao came back out into the bedroom a couple of minutes later. She was now wearing a robe and standing in the middle of the room. It was at the tip of her tongue to ask him to stay again, maybe suggest the light meal and the walk, but she felt a little embarrassed to bring it up. Instead, she followed him silently out to the front foyer and watched as he slipped on his shoes.

"Have a good day," he told her, before pressing a light kiss on her forehead.

He was gone a second later.

Chapter 16

Tao was feeling tense. It was a feeling that had been nagging him for a couple of weeks, and he could not shake it. There were definitely several things that were contributing to the tension. His apartment, for one.

The delay in construction was now more than six weeks long. The wait was getting annoying and he was ready to be in his own space again. It was fine staying with Gary; they were having a good time as roommates. But it was still a big inconvenience for work and his personal life.

Work was definitely a second stress factor. As an independent corporate security consultant for the past two years, Tao had not lacked for jobs. In fact, there had been several occasions in recent months where he was forced to sub out parts of his contracts. He was now at the point where he was considering expanding by establishing a company and hiring one or two consultants to work under him. It was a big decision to make, and it would mean a substantial investment of time and money. He was really excited about the idea but wanted to make sure he had a sound business plan before committing to the venture.

Then there was a third contribution to Tao's recent tension, and her name was Monique Evans. This was the one problem that he had no idea how to fix. Truthfully, he didn't even know how to define it much less find a solution. All he knew was that she occupied way too much of his brain space, and nothing he did seemed to improve the situation.

It was now Thursday evening, and Tao was finishing off some work on his current project. His only plan for the evening was to stop at the grocery store on the way home. Gary was free also, so they would probably grill up some steaks and spend the evening watching television and doing more work.

Ideally, Tao would rather be spending the evening with Monique, but that was not the routine that they had established over the last couple of weeks. They had spoken briefly on Wednesday after the game and confirmed that he would go to her place on Friday. It was what they had done the week before.

Tao had been pretty annoyed when he left her house on the Sunday morning after Nicole's party. It bothered him that she had wanted him to leave after sex. And why had he pretended it was no big deal? He had broken his own rule of honesty, again. Then the more Tao thought about it, the more annoyed he became about Monique's need for rules.

For about a couple of days after the incident, he seriously considered whether the whole thing was really worth it. Yes, it should be every man's dream to have a friend with benefits, but it was turning out to be a little more complicated than he had anticipated. Like the other common male fantasy of a threesome, it was great in theory, but messy and awkward in reality.

He did not call her that week, but as their basketball game approached on Wednesday, Tao felt some pressure to decide how he was going to handle the situation. His first instinct was to just play it cool, and see what direction things took. If Monique seemed interested in hooking up again, that was fine, but he wasn't going to pursue it.

That resolution lasted until she walked into the gym wearing her typical sweat clothes and team jersey. Her hair was pulled back into a ponytail and her face looked freshly washed and clean of makeup. It wasn't her appearance that grabbed his attention and caused a tightening in his throat. It was the memory of how good it felt to touch her skin and kiss her lips.

Tao approached her as she walked toward their team bench. She seemed surprised by his direct attention, but responded to his silent nod with one of her own.

"Is everything cool?" he asked casually, not referring to anything in particular.

"Yeah, everything is good," replied Monique with a slight smile.

"Good," Tao added.

He wanted to start a conversation, just something general, but the whistle blew, indicating that the game would start in a couple of minutes.

"Will you be around for a bit after the game?" he asked her.

Monique nodded, still smiling.

The game was fast-paced and energetic. They had played the opposing team once before and though the Ravens had won, the game had been close. Tonight, Tao's team was not so fortunate. They played okay, but the competition was on fire and the Ravens lost by four points.

Not much was said between the guys as they headed to the shower. The playoffs were coming up just before Christmas, and they were going to have to pull things together if they wanted to do well. Their team was one of the better ones in the league, but the last games were not reflective of their typical abilities. It was clear that every player was getting concerned about what was causing the lack of synergy and performance, and hoping that it would not continue.

While the men were getting dressed, Tao suggested that they all meet a little early the following Wednesday to strategize a bit. Gary was in a rush to leave and was not able to stay around for dinner afterward, so Tao assured him that he would hang around and let Monique know about the plan for next week. Nigel heard the discussion and suggested the rest of them get something to eat, obviously hoping that Monique would be able to join them. Tao quickly said he had other plans, and the others also declined one by one.

When Tao and Gary left the changing room, Monique was not there yet, so Gary continued on. Tao stopped near the main doors of the recreation center where Monique would see him as she came out of the women's changing room. She stepped out a few minutes later and coincidentally met up with Nigel at the same time. Tao could not hear their conversation, but he was sure Nigel asked her to dinner and she said no. More discussion happened, and from the look of determined resolution on her face, and Nigel's slumped shoulders, Tao got the impression that she finally put him out of his misery. Nigel walked away with slow steps but did not look at Tao as he passed him to go outside.

Monique's expression was unreadable when she reached Tao.

"What happened?" he asked as they went outside together.

"He wanted to go to dinner and I said no."

"That's it?"

She let out a deep breath. "No. He wanted to go out sometime this weekend. I told him that I was seeing someone else."

"Really?" replied Tao, his surprise was very obvious.

Monique glanced at him with slight annoyance. "It was the only thing that I could think of to stop him from continuing to try. I could tell he wasn't going to take the hint and stop asking me out."

"Did you tell him who you were seeing?"

Tao had no clue why he asked the question. He knew she hadn't, but he wanted to see how she would respond.

"Of course not!"

"Maybe you should have," he suggested. "I know you think that keeping things on the down-low would be easier, but maybe we should just put it out there so we don't have to be so secretive."

Monique looked at him like he was crazy.

"And how exactly would we explain it? That we're just sex partners? So everyone can think that I'm a total slut?" she demanded.

"No, that's not what I meant," he explained trying to keep his tone very calm and even. "I'm surprised that you would care what they thought, anyway."

"I don't care! But I'm not going to go out of my way to give people the wrong impression about me, either."

Tao shrugged. He knew he was being a bit of an instigator, and he wasn't sure why or what he was hoping to gain from it. But he continued to goad her anyway.

"I'm saying we stop hiding and make it obvious that we are spending time together. We don't have to explain anything beyond that, just let people think whatever they want," he told her.

"Why?"

They had reached Monique's car at the point. She opened the trunk and threw her gym bag into it before slamming it shut. Tao had not responded, so she turned to face him and stare him down. He still didn't answer, so she raised her eyebrows to indicate she was still waiting for an answer.

"Why hide it?" he finally responded.

Monique twisted her mouth in irritation, and Tao shrugged nonchalantly. His cavalier attitude seemed to annoy her even more and she turned away without adding anything else. He felt a wicked twinge of satisfaction, but decided not to push his luck. Once she was sitting in her car, he brought up the subject of the extra practice next week.

"Listen, can you meet a six o'clock next Wednesday instead of seven?" he asked. "The playoffs start in three weeks, so we need to get our asses in gear."

Though her lips were still pinched tight, she nodded to say yes. Tao would have liked to just leave at that point, but he couldn't. He needed to know when they would get together again; that was, of course, if he hadn't pushed her to the point where she would tell him to get lost.

"Are you free on Friday night?" he finally asked.

It took Monique a few seconds to answer him, but she still looked straight ahead.

"No, I have a work thing, unfortunately."

Tao nodded, ready to walk away and forget everything.

"How about Saturday instead?" she asked.

"Okay, Saturday night works," Tao replied. "I'll come by after about seven?"

"All right."

"Okay," he repeated.

She drove away at that point.

They had gotten together on Saturday as planned, and the following Saturday as well. Both times, Tao went to her house and they ate whatever dinner he brought, then they spent the evening watching a bit of television and having sex. Both times, he left soon after their intimacy, without any discussion.

They only spoke a couple of times during the week, and it was only ever to confirm future plans. It appeared that they were falling into a comfortable routine that should satisfy them both. However, almost three weeks later, Tao wasn't feeling very satisfied. He was tense.

Last Sunday, after their last time together, he had woken up fully aroused and filled with the memories of their lovemaking and how incredible it had been. When he finally rolled out of bed, he wanted to call Monique and talk to her about the silly things that dating people tended to talk about. Maybe, he would ask her if she had woken up thinking about him too. But, of course, he didn't call. Nor did he phone her for the rest of the week. Instead, he waited until Wednesday at their basketball game to confirm that they would see each other again this Saturday.

The need for conversation with Monique did not go away. It actually intensified. Tao would be at work, and several times through the day he would wonder what she was doing. Then in the evenings, he wanted to ask her how her day went or tell her something interesting about his. But, of course, that would all go against the rules.

So now, on a Thursday evening, Tao was hanging out with Gary watching television instead of spending time with Monique getting to know her better. And he was tense.

Chapter 17

The week of their basketball tournament was extremely busy. Based on the number of games the Ravens had won during the season, they were scheduled to play in one of two semifinal games. If they won, the championship game would take place right after. At the same time, Tao finally got confirmation that his apartment was finished and he could move in after December 2, the day before their final games. Ideally, it would have been great to take the week off work, but two of his clients had major investigations going on, and his absence was not an option. Tao decided to delay moving into the condo until that Friday.

Despite the couple of weeks where they weren't able to click, the team turned things around pretty quickly. They spent the two games before the finals revisiting their strengths and going back to the basics. Tao left the starting lineup the same but shuffled their bench around a little bit.

Things went well the night of the playoffs. The Ravens were matched against the Bull Dogs in the semifinals and won an easy victory. They then played the Braves in the finals. It was the same team they had lost to a few weeks earlier, but tonight, Tao, Monique, Gary, and the others brought their best performances. The game was hard and aggressive with more than one controversial contact, but the team took home the trophy in the end.

There was a short celebration party at McKenzie's that evening. As captain, Tao bought the first round of drinks, then stayed around for about an hour. He and Monique spoke briefly, very casually and only about the events of the day, before he left the bar. It wasn't until Saturday morning that he realized that they had not made any plans to get together that weekend. At the same time, Tao remembered that he had not told her that his condo was ready, and he was moving in that weekend. In fact, he had slept there for the first time on Friday night.

Tao took some time while still lying on his bare mattress to think about why he had not mentioned his plans to Monique. He remembered the urge to tell her as soon as he got the news. But, of course, he didn't call her. His intention was to tell her when they saw each other last Saturday.

Unfortunately, not much talking ever happened when Tao and Monique got together. They met up once a week, and the minute they finished eating dinner, they were all over each other. It could be hours before they came up for air.

That was why he had never told her about the apartment.

Now he checked his watch and saw that it was only seven o'clock in the morning. It was way too early to call her, so Tao headed into the shower instead.

His cell phone rang a few hours later while he was rearranging some boxes, and he was very surprised to see Monique's number on the display.

"Hi, Tao," she stated once he answered.

"Hey, Monique, how are you doing?"

"I'm all right. How are you?"

"Good," Tao replied. "So, what's going on?"

"Nothing. I just thought I would touch base," stated Monique.

"How long did you guys stay at the pub on Wednesday?"

"Not long. I'm not sure about the others, but Gary and I left right after you did. It was a crazy week at work, so I couldn't stay out too late."

"Is everything okay?"

"Yeah, it's fine," she dismissed. "Just the regular stuff, you know? Not enough time in the day to get everything done."

"I know exactly what you mean," he added, looking around the chaos in his living room.

"Anyway, I just wanted to see if you were coming over later today."

Tao really wanted to say yes, but he knew he had too much to do in the apartment. His goal was to finish the major unpacking by Monday, and he had barely started.

"I can't," he told her, hoping that his regret came across very clearly.

"Oh."

"Yeah. I actually moved into the condo last night, and I have to finish unpacking."

"Oh! You must be so relieved."

Tao smiled and nodded. She sounded really excited and happy for him.

"I am, trust me. I felt like I was waiting forever, even though it was only about two months. But, I have to say it was worth the wait! The contractor did an amazing job with the renovations."

"Was it a big move? Did you have a lot of stuff in storage?" she asked.

"Nah, just the basics, really. I guess it's a byproduct of Navy life. I never really accumulated more than I could carry on my back. All the big stuff was purchased in the last few weeks."

Monique laughed lightly.

"So it was an easy move then?"

"Yeah. But now I have an apartment full of things to be unpacked and arranged. I don't even know where to begin," Tao confessed.

"Do you want some help?"

He had to admit he was surprised and caught completely off guard by her offer.

"I have a few things to do this afternoon, but I can come by after," she continued.

"Okay," he said simply.

"I should be free by about four o'clock."

"Yeah, that would be fine. I might run out to the store, but I should be around."

"Okay. I'll give you a call around three and get the address and directions," suggested Monique.

"Sounds good," he confirmed.

They said their good-byes, then Tao hung up. He then turned around and looked around. His description had been pretty accurate, and he was incredibly relieved that Monique was going to help him out. Boxes were everywhere, some labeled with his personal stuff, others unopened purchases. New furniture was clustered in the living room where the deliverymen had placed them.

Gary had spent the better part of Friday afternoon and evening helping Tao move, but was unavailable today. It never occurred to Tao that there would still be so much to do.

As he walked toward the kitchen, stepping over and around obstacles along the way, his intention was to make breakfast and a cup of coffee. The only thing in his fridge was a loaf of bread, two bottles of beer, and his favorite hot sauce. There was no way to know where the coffee pot was, nor the box with a new set of dishes and mugs. Tao decided to go out for breakfast instead.

His building was located in a well-established area in downtown San Diego. There were lots of food markets, boutique stores, and restaurants. One place in particular had caught Tao's eye a few times. It was a small, casual American food restaurant that advertised breakfast all day and a brunch on Saturdays and Sundays.

It was now almost 11:30, and the place was

fairly busy. He waited about five minutes before being seated near a window with a view of the street. Tao immediately ordered coffee, then opened the menu to review their options. He was trying to decide between eggs with sausage, bacon and home fries, and pancakes with a side order of sausages, when someone walking toward him caught his eye.

At first, he could not make out how he knew her, but her pretty face and smooth dark skin seemed really familiar. Her curvy figure in snug jeans and a pretty blouse also jogged his memory.

The woman caught his glance, and her face lit up with a beautiful smile. She walked over to him, and it was clear that she recognized him right away.

"Hi there," she stated. "It's Tao, right?"

He still didn't remember her name but suddenly knew where they had met.

"Yeah, that right. You're Monique's friend, right? We met at Nicole's party a few weeks ago."

"We did! It's Tammy Wilcox. What are doing around here?" she asked.

"I just moved into an apartment across the street. Everything is still in boxes, so I'm eating out for the next few days," replied Tao with a rueful smile. "Do you live nearby?"

"No, I'm up in North Clairemont. My sister lives downtown, and we sometimes meet here for lunch," explained Tammy. "I'm waiting for her now, actually."

She turned around to check the entrance of the restaurant. Tao looked with her, but no one stood out as a potential sibling.

"Nope! She's late, as usual," Tammy stated.

"Well, feel free to wait for her here. You'll be able to see her when she comes in."

"Okay, thanks."

He had been placed at a table with four chairs. She took a seat in the one directly across from him. The waitress came by and took Tao's order of eggs, over hard, and Tammy ordered a cup of coffee.

"So, how is the basketball team doing?"

"The season is finished. We had the last game and playoffs on Wednesday," he told her.

"Oh. How did you guys do?"

Tao grinned. It was only a recreational house league, but he liked to win.

"We came in first place," he told her, barely able to refrain from grinning.

Tammy laughed.

"That's great! With you, Gary, and Monique on the team, who could beat you guys!"

Tao laughed and lowered his head with humility. Something about the way she said the compliment made him feel as though she might be flirting, and it caught him by surprise.

"Well, we couldn't have done it without Monique, that's for sure. That girl has some serious skills!" he told her.

"So I've heard," replied Tammy.

Tao nodded.

"Oh, there's my sister."

She stood up and waved and immediately got her sister's attention. The woman was a few shades lighter, slightly rounder, and was dressed in less-expensive clothes. But she had the same pretty face and discreet sensuality.

Tao stood up as well.

"Hey sis," she said to Tammy when she reached them.

The two women hugged tightly.

"Tao, this is my sister, Emily. Emily, this Tao Samuels."

"Hi, Emily," he said with a polite nod.

She smiled back, barely hiding her assessing glance up and down his body.

The waitress arrived with Tao's meal and disrupted the group.

"You guys can feel free to join me," he offered. "Unless, you have some women talk you need to do and don't want me to hear."

They all laughed. The girls looked at each other, speaking through their eyes. They then sat in the chairs across from his. As regulars at the restaurant, they knew what they wanted and placed their lunch orders quickly.

The discussion was very casual, starting with Tammy explaining how she knew Tao, then he told them a little about moving into his apartment and being new to living downtown. Emily had moved there more than three years ago and loved it. She lived with her boyfriend in another condo development nearby, and she turned out to be a wealth of knowledge about the area.

The conversation eventually moved to a discussion between the two girls about family issues and obligations. Tao sat back and listened, enjoying the comedic banter between them. They were obviously very smart and articulate; Tammy was a lawyer, and Emily worked in one of the large banks, but they were also funny and down to earth. They teased each other the way normal siblings did, but they were obviously very close and spent a lot of time together.

"Is it just the two of you, or do you have more brothers and sisters?" he asked after they told a really funny story about a recent family event.

"We have an older sister, Janet. She lives up in Oceanside," Tammy told him.

"She's living the suburban life," Emily added with a bit of sarcasm. "A housewife with three kids."

"Yeah, and a little out of touch with the rest of the world," added Tammy.

The woman exchanged knowing looks, and Tao could tell right away that there was some friction there.

"You guys aren't close?" he asked.

"We used to be as kids," Tammy replied. "Janet is only one year older than me, three years older than Emily. But she got married at nineteen and turned into someone else overnight. I love her to death and my nephews are the cutest kids ever, but she has no interests outside of her family. And don't get me started on her husband."

Emily nodded with agreement. It was clear that Janet was a regular discussion point.

"What's wrong with him?" he asked.

"He's not a bad guy. He's just not really there. You know, always working, distant, totally self-involved. And it just makes Janet try harder to please him and make him happy. I honestly think he just married a young girl to get a slave at home and give him some kids. And, now it's like she afraid that if she gets a life or develops an interest outside of the house, he'll get rid of her."

"And there is no point talking to Janet about it. We've tried, which is why she doesn't really talk to us that much anymore," added Emily. "She thinks she has a fairytale life and the perfect, hardworking husband. It's like she worships the ground he walks on. I actually get nauseated watching them together."

"Wow," replied Tao.

"Sad, huh?" suggested Tammy. "It's not that I'm against marriage or anything, but that's not my idea of how it should be."

She spoke while looking at Tao speculatively. It was a look he immediately recognized, but did not return. Tammy was letting him know her views on relationships for a reason. He decided to change the subject to something more casual.

"So, were you guys raised in San Diego?"

"Pretty much," Emily told him.

They spent the rest of the hour or so at the restaurant, talking more about growing up in California. Tao shared a little about his life with his mom in Bakersfield, and being half Chinese Jamaican and half African American. It was an interesting explanation of Chinese culture in the Caribbean, and of how his mother immigrated to the United States to work in a refinery. The women were completely fascinated and asked questions long after their meals were finished.

Finally, Tao left Tammy and her sister to head back to his errands and the unpacking that needed to be done at the apartment. While doing his grocery shopping at a market that Emily had recommended, he did some thinking about the time spent with the two women. During the course of a meal, he had revealed more about his family and life than he had ever discussed with Monique. How did that happen? Was it only because they had asked? And what did it mean about his relationship with Monique?

Chapter 18

Monique called Cara right after she hung up with Tao. The women were supposed to have lunch together then go shopping at Fashion Valley Mall. They arranged to meet at twelve-thirty in front of the Cheesecake Factory. Cara was already there when Monique arrived and they were seated quickly at a table.

"Where are the girls?" Monique asked her once they had placed their meal orders. "I thought you were going to bring them."

"I was, but Kyle went to see his parents and his mom wouldn't hear of him not bringing the kids to visit," explained Cara. "And to be honest, I wasn't looking forward to shopping with them today. Meghan's in the really difficult stage where she touches everything and flops on the floor every time she doesn't get what she wants. I'm not in the mood to be embarrassed while she screams her head off."

"Well, she's almost two, right? That's normal, isn't it?"

"Yeah, it's normal, but it doesn't mean I have to like it. Maddie was the same, but it gives me a headache to deal with it. Maybe someone can take her away and just bring her back when she turns three."

"Don't look at me!" exclaimed Monique with a laugh. "I love Meghan to death, but I'm not ready for kids yet, that's for sure."

"That's true. You would just give her everything she wants to keep her quiet. She would be completely spoiled when you brought her back, and I would have to spend the next ten years deprogramming her!" Cara added.

"That's right. My role as Godmother is to spoil them rotten, then give them back to you and go home."

"Nice!"

They laughed together. Their food arrived shortly after, and discussion changed to an update on what was going on with Cara's life. She told Monique that everything was as busy as usual but going well. The only problem was that Kyle was now spending several days a week in Los Angeles doing consulting work for a private hospital.

"He's always traveled, so I understand it. But this is the first time he's done it like this. I mean, he now leaves early Monday morning and doesn't come back until Wednesday evening, sometimes even Thursday. It's almost like he has another life there, you know?"

"Well, Cara, LA is a two-hour drive. It's not practical for him to commute every day," reasoned Monique.

"I know, I know. I'm not trying to be unreasonable. And yes, I have plenty of help with the nanny. I guess I just miss him, that's all. But this is what I signed up for when I decided to marry a surgeon, right? And I have always tried to support his ambitions and the growth of his career. It's a little late to complain about it now. Or, at least that's what I keep telling myself."

Monique didn't respond. They had had this conversation on many occasions as Cara struggled with the reality of her marriage to Kyle. The long hours while he was an intern, then in residence, and more recently, the travel and commitment to his clinic.

"I'm not sure what makes this any different, Monique, but I feel like it is. I've even started to wonder if there is another reason why he wants to be in LA regularly."

It took Monique a few seconds to pick up on what Cara was implying.

"You mean, like a woman?" she asked incredulously. "Are you serious, Cara?"

"I don't know," her friend moaned. "It's crazy, right? Kyle is just not the type to cheat. Or maybe that's just what I tell myself. Every man is the type to cheat given the opportunity, right?"

Monique shrugged. "I don't know. I think some people, men and women, will cheat if they believe they can get away with it. But not everyone. I also think some people do it because they can justify their reasons, right? Their spouse isn't doing this or that. Or they don't feel loved anymore, or they're not getting enough attention at home. In the end, it's just an excuse to have their cake and eat it too. But, then again, I have a different perspective on married men who cheat. So maybe I'm not the best person to have this conversation with, Cara."

Her tone wasn't bitter or despondent, only realistic.

"No, you are the best person to talk to, Monique. I watched you try to deal with it from the other side, and it made me see that things like cheating aren't a black and white issue. I used to think it was just about right and wrong, but there are so many grey areas," Cara replied. "I guess women like me like to believe in black and white because the alternative is scary. Is it possible for our husbands to love us and love their families, but still be capable of having sexual and intimate relationships with other women? That is a really hard reality to accept, and it makes knowing whether to leave or stay an even harder decision."

"Okay, Cara, slow down. Kyle is not cheating, so you don't have to make any decisions. You guys are fine. Kyle is not Donald Sanderson. Not even close."

"How do you know? Donald maintained a relationship with you for three years and still never left his wife. How do you know his wife wasn't completely happy and satisfied with her life, not knowing what he was doing on the side? You don't even know if they were ever going to get separated. You only know what he told you, right?"

"I know," Monique echoed, trying not to get defensive. "I don't know the truth, and I probably never will. I didn't seek to break up his marriage, Cara. It's not like I met him at work knowing he was married, then enticed him into a relationship hoping that he would leave her. He pursued me, and from the beginning he was adamant that they were technically separated, that he was getting ready to move out. It seemed harmless, like if I met someone who was already separated and just waiting for the official paperwork. I don't know why I believed him, but I did for a long time. And I will always regret that."

"I'm sorry, Monique. I'm not trying to make this about you. Really! It's just, after seeing what you went through, it's scary to see what people are capable of, men in particular!"

"I know," replied Monique. "But at the same time, don't let it make you crazy, or make you see things that aren't there. Why don't you go with him to LA for a couple of days? You can do some shopping, go to a spa. Then you can see for yourself what's going on."

"I guess," Cara agreed, though she still sounded skeptical. "Anyway, let's change the subject. We're supposed to be having fun, so enough depressing talk. I got a call from Melissa last night, all upset. She finally broke up with Jones."

"Good! He sounded like a real loser. Did you ever find out if that is his first name or last name?"

They both laughed out loud.

"No. I don't think Mel knows either. Anyway, she's all depressed now, wondering why she can't find the right guy for her. I keep telling her that she makes the worst choices, but it's like talking to a brick wall."

"She sounds exactly like Gary. His taste in women is just as bad."

"Hey, maybe we should hook them up?" Cara suggested. "It's been a while since I've seen him, but he seemed like a good guy."

Cara had met Gary a few years back, while Monique was still in school.

"It's funny you would say that. He met Tammy a few weeks ago and it looked like it was love at first sight," Monique told her.

"No way! So, are they dating now?"

"I don't know. Gary hasn't said much, and I haven't spoken to Tammy in a couple of weeks. But to be honest, I really can't see them together. They are attractive, smart people with stable careers, but they both prefer to date losers with issues and drama."

Cara burst out laughing, and Monique eventually joined her.

"In that case, my sister might be perfect for him, except in her relationships, she is the stable one! If he doesn't hook up with Tammy, let's get him together with Melissa."

They laughed some more and continued to discuss the dating decisions of the people in their lives.

Once they finished their meals, they left the restaurant and spent more than two hours in a few of their favorite department stores. Eventually, Cara brought up the only topic they hadn't already discussed.

"So? How are things going with Tao?"

Monique smiled a little and looked away while shrugging.

"Pretty much the same."

"Oh, give me a break!"

"I'm serious! We're still seeing each other, you know, casually. But that's it."

"So, why the goofy grin? I mentioned his name and your eyes lit up like a Christmas tree."

"Oh, shut up!" demanded Monique, barely able to contain an embarrassed giggle.

"Come on! Cough up the real deal," Cara insisted.

"Nothing has changed. But, it's been really good. We get along well . . ."

"And?"

Monique let out a deep breath. "And . . . I can't stop thinking about him! I don't mean the sex either. That's great. Phenomenal actually. But, I can't stop thinking about his smile, or something funny he said, or the way he plays ball. It's insane, and very, very annoying!"

Cara burst out with a long giggle of her own.

"I know," Monique lamented. "I'm starting to realize that my brilliant plan for a casual friend with benefits may not be such a good idea after all."

"You think?"

The simple words were dripping with sarcasm. Monique shot her a cutting glare, but Cara just shrugged, completely unaffected.

"What are you going to do?" she asked Monique.

"I don't know. Continue to enjoy things, I guess. It's a little too late to change the rules now, considering I was the one to create them to begin with. Well, most of them anyway."

"What do you mean? Tao had rules too?"

"It seems silly now, but I insisted that the whole thing would only work if we agreed on a few things. Like rules of engagement, you know? I said it had to be casual, exclusive, and with no romantic expectations. He added honesty."

"Really?" Cara asked.

"Yeah. Odd, isn't it? Who expects honesty in a casual thing? But, that's how he is. He says exactly what he's thinking no matter how private and intimate. It's a little unnerving."

"Well, then, you have no choice."

"What do you mean?" Monique asked, a little lost in the direction of their conversation.

"You have to be honest and tell him that you've changed your mind and you want to try a more meaningful relationship with him."

"Wait! I didn't say all of that."

"Monique Evans, I have been your best friend since we were seven years old. You don't have to say all that for me to know that's exactly what you want."

Chapter 19

Monique parted ways with Cara at the mall and headed straight to Tao's new apartment. She called him on the way from her car to get directions and arrived around three-thirty in the afternoon. His building was a highrise, glass and steel pillar in a beautiful spot on Market Street. It was still under construction, but about 80 percent complete. She parked on the street around the corner then walked back, stopping at a market along the way to pick up a nice potted plant as a housewarming gift.

As Monique rode up in the elevator, she got increasingly nervous. Cara's words echoed in her mind. Her advice was really good, but easier said than done. The idea of telling Tao that she had changed her mind and would like to throw out all the rules that she had been so adamant about only a few weeks ago made Monique feel a little nauseated.

She found his apartment very easily, and Tao opened the door after her first knock. They had just seen each other on Wednesday at their playoff games, yet looking at him immediately caused a physical reaction in her stomach.

"You made it," he said with a smile.

"Hi, Tao. Yeah, I made it okay. It was pretty easy to find," she replied with a smile of her own.

He stepped aside and she walked into the apartment. It was a loft-style with high ceilings and an open-concept floor plan. Monique immediately saw why Tao waited to move in until the renovations he'd requested were done. There were many extra features, from the beautiful dark bamboo floors to custom blinds and walls painted in warm grey. There were also boxes and furniture piled up everywhere.

"Tao, this is such a great space. How many square feet is it?"

"Just under one thousand. It looks bigger because of the high ceiling."

"I thought you said you didn't have a lot of stuff," she teased.

He laughed easily.

"That's what I thought, but looking at it now, I don't even know what's in all these boxes."

She laughed also, and walked over to stand in front of him.

"Well, I guess it's a good thing that I'm here to help you out, huh? I hope you will make it worth my while."

Tao chuckled again, showing that he enjoyed her flirting. He pulled her into the circle of his arms and placed a soft, sensual kiss on her waiting lips. The embraced stretched out longer than they had both anticipated as neither appeared ready to end it.

"Hmm," he mumbled. "I will compensate you any way you want."

Monique giggled, and they kissed again briefly.

"Okay, let's get to work," she commanded. "What room do you want to start in?"

Tao chose the kitchen, and the two of them started searching through his things for the appropriate items.

They continued to work in harmony, moving from the kitchen to the living room and finally to his bedroom and master bathroom. Monique was making the bed while Tao unpacked the items for his shower. He stepped into the bedroom, rolling his shoulders to relieve some tightness.

"What time is it?" he asked.

They had yet to find his alarm clock or his watch.

"Almost eight o'clock," she replied after checking her own watch and looking out the dark windows. "Wow, I can't believe how late it is."

"I can!" protested Tao, now rubbing a spot in the back of his neck. "We've been at this for hours. I'm starving. Are you hungry?"

Monique did a mental calculation of the time since her lunch, and her stomach grumbled in response.

"I am, actually," she told him.

"Okay. Let's go get some air and find somewhere to eat."

She finished covering his pillows while Tao changed into jeans and a cotton shirt. They left a few minutes later to walk down his street toward the bay. There were quite a few restaurants and hotels, and they picked one that looked fun inside and had a casual menu. They sat down and ordered beers and a pizza that they could share.

"Are you going to miss rooming with Gary?" Monique asked.

"Nah. Gary is a great guy, and we get along all right, but I like living alone," he told her. "I've bunked and roomed with God knows how many servicemen over the years. I lived by myself for the first time when I moved to San Diego. It was a little weird at first; quiet. But I got used to it eventually."

"I know what you mean," she added. "I grew up in a small house with lots of big men. My bedroom was the size of a closet, but it was mine. Even my college dorms were a luxury. So, when I found my house, it was like living a dream I had never dared to have."

Tao nodded, listening quietly but also letting her know he understood where she was coming from.

"Have you been back to Detroit recently?" he asked.

"No, not since I left. My brothers came to visit me last year for a week. My parents are pretty stubborn and set in their ways. They have no interest in traveling anywhere beyond Ann Arbor."

She smiled wryly, and Tao grinned back.

Their pizza arrived. Monique took the opportunity to change the subject and asked him about some of the places he went during his tours of duty. She then listened intently while he talked for the next hour, describing some of the most exotic cities in the world. When they left the restaurant, they walked around the grounds of the hotel nearby then down toward the bay. At some point, Tao took her hand in his. They were fully engrossed in their discussion, and had no destination in mind. Eventually, they ended up on the boardwalk leading to Seaport Village, a large open outdoor shopping complex on the waterfront. It was absolutely beautiful at night. There was a break in the conversation as they both looked out over the calm water. The December breeze was cool. Monique was wearing just cotton pants and a zippered sweatshirt, though, and she shivered at the feel of it. Tao pulled her close and wrapped his arm around her waist.

"This is a beautiful spot. When I was stationed at the naval base, between tours, I used run to here and back almost every day," he told her.

"Really? Isn't that really far?"

"It's not bad, about three miles. I was in better shape then," he joked.

"That's right. Now you're an old man with limited capacity," Monique teased back.

"Hey now! That's not funny."

They laughed together for a few seconds, then enjoyed the view for several more minutes before starting the walk back to his place. There was a comfortable silence for most of the way.

When they got inside, Tao pulled Monique into a hug.

"Thanks for your help today, Monique. God

knows how long it would have taken me to get all this done by myself."

"You're welcome," she replied simply.

"I suppose, now you want your compensation, huh?"

"We did have an agreement. But, since you're in such bad physical shape, I'll understand if you're too exhausted to deliver."

"Oh, man! Don't you know that you should never question a man's capability to perform certain duties? Now I'm going to have to prove my abilities."

Tao twisted his face to seem truly injured.

"That's right," she told him, continuing the teasing banter. "And if you don't perform to my standards, you'll just have to do it all over again."

His eyes lit up at the idea, and they both smiled at their silliness. He then leaned forward to kiss her gently. Monique responded immediately, engaging his lips, teasing his flesh with the edge of her teeth. Tao swept his tongue along the inner edge of her mouth, dipping inside to taste her sweetness. She moaned, extending her tongue to play with his.

After a lengthy embrace, Tao pulled away to take her hand and lead them to his bedroom, now lit only by the moonlight streaming through his windows. They fell onto the bed, still kissing while their hands began exploring each other's bodies. He unzipped her sweatshirt, gently pulled it off her arms, and tossed it aside. Monique was wearing a simple white T-shirt underneath. The thin fabric could not conceal her aroused breasts as they strained against her bra. He enveloped them in his hand, exploring their firm shape while his mouth continued to ravish hers.

Monique felt breathless from the sensations he created in her body. She stroked the hard contours of his shoulders and back, occasionally running her fingers through the short crop of his hair.

"Take off your top," whispered Tao.

She complied immediately, eager to be naked to his touch. Monique threw her T-shirt and bra to the floor, then lay back down on the bed. When his lips left hers to make their way down to her straining nipples, she bit her bottom lip to hold back the moans. Soft gasps escaped her lips as he bathed the sensitive buds with his tongue, occasionally sucking one then the other into his mouth until she wanted to scream.

Finally, she sat up, reaching for Tao's pants with urgent need. He took her suggestion and stood up to slide them down his legs. Monique could not take her eyes of his hard, straining flesh, but she used the opportunity to strip off her panties. When he joined her on the bed, she flipped their position so he lay face up, and she could straddle his hips.

His look of surprise was visible in the moonlight and quickly changed to delight. Monique grinned back at him as she ran her fingers down his chest.

"I'm really liking this view," she told him breathlessly.

Tao nodded with a goofy smile on his face.

"I'm thinking it's my new favorite," he replied.

She continued to stoke the contours of his chest and abdomen, working her way down to the base of his stomach. He could not take his eyes off of her, but his breathing became shallow and fast. The lower she reached, the more he quivered. Then Monique encircled his straining erection with her hands. Tao's breath came out in a long hiss.

His large hands gripped her hips, lifting her effortlessly and positioning her for his possession. He then lowered her slowly, encasing himself in her tight wetness. They both froze in the moment, overwhelmed with intense sensations.

"Tao," Monique mumbled with her face buried in the side of his neck.

"Oh, baby," he echoed.

With his hands still holding her firmly, Tao gently started to thrust deep into her center, using long, maddening strokes. They got lost in the moment, allowing their bodies to set the pace. Their groans started out soft and rhythmic, and escalated to loud, shuddering cries and they climaxed together.

Tao held her close, still encased in her warmth, then rolled them together on their sides and pulled up the sheets until they were covered. They fell asleep almost immediately.

When they both stirred again, it was sometime in the morning and sunlight flooded the room. Tao pulled Monique close to him so that her back fit tightly against his torso. They both wiggled a bit, expelling sleeping moans until they found a comfortable position to doze for several more minutes.

"Good morning," he finally said, kissing her softly on her shoulder.

"Hey," she mumbled while rolling on her back. "What time is it?"

Tao stayed on his side and looked down at her with sleepy eyes.

"I'm not sure," he admitted.

Monique blinked a few times to get used to the sunlight. She was then clear-minded enough to check her watch.

"Oh! It's seven-fifteen," she told him with her brows furrowed in thought.

"Hmm," he replied, nonchalantly. "It's early. Do you have to be somewhere?"

"No," admitted Monique, relaxing a bit. "I was just thinking that I hadn't planned to stay over. I don't have anything with me."

Tao placed another kiss on the top of her arm, using his tongue to tease her skin.

"I'm sure I can find an extra toothbrush somewhere."

His tone was very teasing and Monique smiled up at him. He pulled her close so that their bodies were spooned again.

"I had a nice time yesterday," he said, speaking softly near her ear.

"I did too."

They lay together quietly under the sheets, enjoying the warmth from their naked bodies and allowing their thoughts to wander is various directions.

"I'm thinking about having a little get-together soon. Before Christmas. I'm thinking next Saturday. What do you think? Is that too soon?" suggested Tao.

"One week? Will you have enough time to get the apartment in order and finish unpacking?" she asked.

"Yeah, I think so. There's not much left to do now. And anything still in boxes will just be shoved under the bed."

Monique rolled her eyes, thinking he was such a typical man.

"Okay. Well, let me know if you need any help," she offered.

Chapter 20

Arranging his housewarming party was easier than Tao had anticipated. The few get-togethers he had in his old apartment had been casual and last minute, usually with just a few guys watching the Superbowl or the NBA finals. Monique suggested it would be easier if he did something that started later in the evening and served only drinks and appetizers. He took her suggestion and found a local restaurant that would deliver several platters of finger food, and then he picked up a few bottles of wine and a case of beer.

Tao invited about twenty of his friends, including the guys on the basketball team, Anthony and his wife, Jason and Isaac, and a couple of people he worked with in the last couple of years. He told them to bring a guest if they liked, and based on the responses, he was expecting around forty people. If they all showed up, it would be a little crowded but not uncomfortable.

He also spent the days prior to the party doing as much unpacking and settling in as possible.

Monique came by twice after work and helped out with whatever was needed. By seven-thirty the night of his housewarming, it looked pretty good.

Tao was brushing his hair when he heard the first knock at his door. Though he had told everyone to arrive at eight o'clock, he was still surprised to see that it was only eight-fifteen. His expectation was that no one would really come until at least nine o'clock.

The first guest turned out to be Tammy.

Tao had anticipated that Monique would invite her friend, so when Tao ran into Tammy in the area a few days earlier he had extended an invitation to her and her sister. She was standing in the doorway alone.

They had a warm welcome, including a quick hug and kisses on the cheek.

"Where is your sister?" Tao asked once she was inside.

"Emily couldn't make it. She went out of town for the weekend," Tammy explained.

She handed him her jacket and Tao hung it in the closet. When he turned back around, it was to find her wearing a flowing, short black dress with an Empire waist and a square neckline that revealed most of her assets.

"Where is everyone?" she asked looking around.

"You're the first," he told her as he walked past her farther into the apartment. "Would you like a drink?"

"Sure. What do you have?"

Tao stepped into the kitchen and Tammy followed close behind.

"Red or white wine, beer, sodas?" he suggested.

"I'll have some red wine."

She leaned with one hip against the counter while Tao uncorked the bottle of shiraz and poured her a glass. Her gaze was steady and direct as she accepted the drink.

"So, do I get a tour of your place?" she asked before taking the first sip.

Tao was certain he was not imagining her seductive pose or the interest in her eyes. He laughed to himself, still a little surprised by the vibes he got from her.

"Sure," he replied politely.

He took her on a brief walk around the condo, pointing out a couple of things, like the view of the bay from the living room, his empty second bedroom, then the master bedroom and en suite bath, and, finally, the powder room near the front entrance.

"I remember when they started building this place. I can't believe it's finished so quickly. Did you buy this unit from a floor plan?" she asked when they returned to the living room.

"No, I bought it as a resale a few months ago," he explained.

Their conversation was interrupted by another knock. It was Scott and Nigel, followed closely by Gary with Jason and Isaac. Within thirty minutes, there were about twenty-five people at the party. Monique was one of the last to arrive. Tao was busy handing out drinks in the kitchen, so Gary answered the door for him.

Tao heard several people welcome her, then he saw her the second she entered the living room and into his line of vision. He let out a deep breath, realizing how much he had been anticipating her presence and wondering when she would arrive. She spotted him too, smiled, and waved her fingers at him. She then passed two bottles of wine to him over the kitchen counter.

One hour later, the party was in full swing with everyone talking and laughing in small groups. Soft music played in the background, and the food and drinks were flowing. Tao had talked briefly and casually with Monique with others around, and shared lots of eye contact with her, but he had yet to be with her alone. They were still acting as though they were friends and nothing else.

Tao was not certain why that surprised him. Yes, he and Monique had spent more quality time together over the past week. In his mind, there had been a change after that first night in his apartment. Technically, the rules of their relationship were still in place, but he had started to feel that the rules were no longer relevant.

Now, as he played bartender in the kitchen again, and watched her chatting with Tammy across the room near the balcony, Tao wondered why they were still hiding their relationship from their friends. He wanted to go over to her now, wrap his arms around her waist, and press an intimate kiss at that sweet spot behind her ear. He almost smiled as he imagined her shocked reaction.

Gary came over and stood beside Tao at that moment and followed the direction of Tao's gaze.

"That girl really knows how to wear a dress," stated Gary.

Monique was wearing black pants and a white camisole-style top, so Tao assumed Gary was referring to Tammy.

"Whatever happened between you two?" he asked Gary. "Last I remember, it was love at first sight."

Gary shrugged.

"Nothing happened. I gave her my number, but she never called me."

"Really? Did you guys talk at all tonight? Are you still interested?"

"We said hi, and chatted a bit, but I'm not gonna go there. She's great to look at and everything, but a little out of my league, I think. You, know: high maintenance."

Tao nodded.

"It's funny, but Monique thought Tammy had come with me, and asked me the same thing a little while ago," continued Gary. "I guess the two of them haven't talked in a while."

"No, I invited her. I ran into her a few days ago and told her about it," Tao explained. "Her sister lives nearby and I've seen them around. I just assumed that Monique would bring her anyway."

Gary nodded.

"Well, it's a pretty good turnout tonight. Everyone seems to be having a good time," Gary commented.

"Yeah, it's not bad. I'm almost out of food, but otherwise it's going pretty smoothly."

Both Monique and Tammy looked over at the two men at that moment, and it was clear that the women had been talking about them. Gary nudged Tao and wiggled his eyebrows.

"It looks like you're the topic of their conversation, Tao. How long are you and Monique going to pretend there's nothing going on between you?"

Tao resisted the urge to look surprised at Gary's comments. He knew that it was hard for him to take his eyes off Monique all night. Gary was probably not the only person to take note of his distracted attention. Now that it was out in the open, Tao was relieved to be able to discuss it with his friend.

"Hey, it's all Monique's idea. She's got it in her head that it's less complicated if we keep things quiet. I don't really care who knows," he explained.

"Is it serious?" Gary asked.

"It wasn't supposed to be, but it's getting there. At least for me, anyway. I'm not sure what she's thinking right now."

Gary patted him on the shoulder.

"Well, give her some time. It might take her a while to adjust to the idea of something significant again."

Tao nodded, looking over at Monique again.

Their eyes met and clung for a few seconds. He quickly poured a couple more glasses of wine and walked over to where she stood.

"Hey," he said when he reached the two women.

"There you are," Tammy replied.

Her face lit up with a bright smile, and she leaned toward him slightly. Tao knew immediately that she was more than a little tipsy.

"I'm staying at my sister's apartment tonight. Maybe we can have breakfast together again tomorrow," she continued with a silly giggle.

Her tone implied something very intimate, and Tao's brow furrowed with confusion. He looked at Monique and opened his mouth, ready to clarify Tammy's statement.

"Excuse me," whispered Monique.

She abruptly turned and walked away, her eyes dark and unreadable. He started to follow her, but was stopped by a firm hand on his wrist.

"Oh, I don't feel so well, Tao," Tammy confessed. "Can you take me to your bedroom? I think I should lie down for a minute."

Tao looked toward Monique, then back down at the drunk woman that was swaying a little. He decided that putting Tammy in his room where it was quiet and dark was a good idea. He would also point out the bathroom to her in case she need to throw up or something. Then, he could go find Monique.

He took Tammy by the wrist and worked his way through the crowd with her trailing behind. Once in his bedroom, he kept the light off and sat her on the bed. Tao then turned on the bathroom light. She leaned to one side and looked as though she was about to fall onto her side. He walked back to her and straightened her with his hand lightly on her shoulders.

"Tammy, are you okay?" he asked, now more concerned. "Do you want some water? Coffee?"

She shook her head to say no.

"How are you feeling?" he probed.

She giggled and put her hands up so they fell on his stomach. "I'm fine, Tao. I'm just feeling a little fuzzy."

He was about to leave her there, satisfied that she would not come to any harm, but she suddenly stood up and awkwardly fell toward him. Her arms landed around his neck, and Tao instinctively gripped her waist to steady her. She then pulled his head down and kissed him on the lips.

He froze for a couple of seconds, completely surprised by her actions. Finally, he pulled away and forcibly pried her fingers away from the back on his shoulders.

"Come on, baby. I know you want me," she breathed.

"Tammy, you're drunk," he said gently but firmly. "You don't know what you're saying."

"You don't have to pretend, Tao. I can give you what you want," she continued, as though he hadn't spoken.

Tao got her to sit down.

"Look, feel free to stay in here as long as you need to. Maybe lie down, sleep if off? I'll ask Gary to drive you home later."

She giggled again. "Okay, I'll wait here for you."

Tao just shook his head, frustrated at his attempt to reason with her inebriated mind. He left the bedroom, closing the door behind him, and went to search for Gary and Monique. Gary was still in the kitchen, nibbling on the last of the cheese and crackers, but Monique was nowhere to be found.

"Hey, have you seen Monique?" he asked Gary.

"She just left."

"What? Why?" demanded Tao while still looking around the apartment.

Gary shrugged. "I don't know. She just said she had to go, then headed out the door. Is everything okay?"

"She didn't say anything?"

"No," Gary told him.

Tao slammed his hand on the counter, cursing with frustration. Several people turned to look at him with surprise, but he barely noticed. Instead, he rushed to the front door and flung it open, leaving Gary to stare after him. But the hallway was empty. Monique was gone. He swore again, pounding his fist on the wall. The feeling at the pit of his stomach told him that he knew exactly why she had taken off without saying good-bye.

Chapter 21

"Are you sure that's what you saw?" Cara asked.

It was Sunday, early afternoon. Monique had gone to Cara's house for breakfast, and they were sitting in her kitchen having coffee. Kyle was in the family room watching a movie with the girls.

"Absolutely! They were in his bedroom kissing," Monique replied in an emotionless voice.

"Wow. I just can't believe that Tammy would do that. Or Tao for that matter. What the hell is going on?"

Monique shrugged.

"The weird thing is that he and I were starting to get closer. At least, that's what I thought. But maybe it was my imagination," she stated. "It turns out that he and Tammy had been seeing each other the whole time."

"What?"

"Yup. She and I haven't really talked in a few weeks, so I was pretty surprised to see her there last night. Then, I thought maybe she and Gary had started dating and she had come with him. But Gary said they never even spoke on the phone."

"So, how did she hear about it?" Cara asked.

"Tao invited her. You should have seen her face when she told me. I mean, I knew that Tammy was ruthless, I've seen her in action at work. But, I just never imagined she could be like that with me. We weren't best friends or anything, but still!"

"Nothing surprises me anymore. People are capable of lots of nasty things. I just don't understand why she targeted Tao. He's not her typical drama case."

"I don't know," Monique replied. "She didn't seem at all interested in him when they met. Like I said, she was too busy flirting with Gary. That was the night I told her that Tao and I were seeing each other casually."

"Well, maybe that's it," Cara concluded. "Maybe she saw him as a challenge. Like she could get him if she offered him more?"

"That's just ugly."

The two women looked down at the table, digesting the reality of the situation.

"How are you feeling?" Cara finally asked.

Monique rubbed her hands over her eyes. After a night spent crying, they felt puffy and gritty.

"I feel like I've been punched in the stomach."

Cara took her hand and squeezed it. The small bit of comfort made Monique's eyes well up with tears again. She bit her lip, trying to control the trembling.

"It really took me by surprise, Cara. I wanted

something casual so that I wouldn't ever feel like this again, like my heart was being ripped out of my chest. And here I am."

The last sentence came out with a sob.

"I can't explain it but it hurts more than it did when I finally ended it with Donald. Bizarre, I know! But, that whole thing was so full of drama and uncertainty that the end was actually a relief in a way. And I could look back and be angry about his lies and manipulations. But, with Tao, I thought things were getting better, growing, headed somewhere. I was ready to get rid of those stupid rules and tell him that I wanted a relationship. Then, boom! It's all gone."

She wiped away the tears that were pouring down her face, but it didn't stop the flow. Cara squeezed her hand harder.

"I am so sorry, Monique. You don't deserve this."

Monique let out a sharp laugh.

"I don't know, maybe this is karma and I do deserve it! Donald was someone's husband, and I wanted him for myself. I'm not exactly in a position to criticize Tammy, am I?"

"You know it's different. Donald's wife was not your friend. He's the one that betrayed his marriage, not you."

Monique didn't reply, but she squeezed her eyes tight.

"I can't believe how much this hurts. I'm not ready to stop seeing him, being with him. I can't even imagine not spending our weekends together. I already feel so alone. I don't want to be alone again, Cara."

The tears were now flowing freely and she openly sobbed in her pain. It took her a minute or so before she could talk clearly again.

"But, I don't have a choice. It's over. I'll just have to get over him and move on," she stated, trying to sound firm. "Right?"

"Right!" Cara confirmed. "And, you're not alone, okay? Tao Samuels is a dog who is not good enough for you. You're better off without him, even though it hurts now."

"Okay."

Monique stayed in La Jolla for another hour. She and Cara eventually joined Kyle and the kids in the family room to watch the movie playing and spend time with the kids. She would have stayed longer, but seeing the happy family unit was making her even weepier.

The drive back to Mission Bay was a blur. Talking to Cara about the situation had helped but it also made it impossible for Monique to stop thinking about it. The image of Tao holding and kissing Tammy seemed to be permanently etched in her brain.

Monique pulled into her driveway, and sat in the car for a couple of minutes. The rest of the day stretched before here like a dark tunnel. She rubbed the aching spot at the base of her stomach, trying to relieve the nausea and knot that only seemed to be getting worse. Finally, she went into the house and straight into her bedroom, where she climbed under the sheets and tucked the covers around her. She wasn't sleepy, just extremely tired and sluggish.

Maybe if she went to sleep, the day would go by without her having to think about him, yearn for his voice, ache for his touch. Maybe she would wake up on Monday and be completely over him, ready to forget what they had shared. Maybe.

Monique looked at the phone and remembered the message he had left for her that morning. She had been in the shower, crying uncontrollably, when the phone rang, and she'd been in no shape to talk to him. The message he left had been simple and brief, but his voice was serious.

"Monique, it's me. Give me a call when you get this so we can talk. Bye."

She never called him back. She couldn't handle the confrontation right now. Just the thought of hearing him tell her that he wanted Tammy made Monique feel like hyperventilating. Or worse, he would lie about everything and deny what she saw with her own eyes. Then Monique would have to hate him while resisting the urge to believe him.

She snuggled deeper under the sheets, seeking comfort and heat. Her emotional exhaustion finally took its toll, and Monique fell into a dead sleep. She woke up in the early evening, ate a small meal strictly out of necessity, then went back to bed. Unfortunately, Monday morning was no different. She still felt forlorn and adrift.

The next few days passed with aching slowness. There were a few more calls from Tao on her cell

208 *Sophia Shaw*

phone and at home, but no more messages. Monique looked at his number with longing, but could not bring herself to call him back. Then, on Wednesday evening, she made the mistake of answering her phone without checking the caller.

It was almost ten-thirty, and she was stretched out on the couch with the news playing in the background.

"Hello," she said.

"Hey, Monique. It's Tao."

Monique froze, shocked at the sound of his voice. She quickly sat up, and attempted to gather her composure.

"Are you there?" he asked after a long pause.

"I'm here."

He let out a long breath.

"I've been trying to reach you for the last few days. But I guess you know that." She didn't say anything. "I wish you hadn't left so quickly on Saturday. I would have explained what happened with Tammy."

"What is there to explain?"

"Nothing! There's nothing to explain. I know how it must have looked. But she was drunk and I was putting her on the bed to sleep it off. She just kissed me out of the blue."

"Just out of the blue," she mimicked in a sarcastic tone.

"Monique, think about it. Why would I be kissing her in my bedroom with a party full of people in the next room, including you? It doesn't make any sense."

"Why not? You're a single, available guy. You've

been hooking up with her for brunch. You invited her to your party. And she's pretty hot and obviously into you. It makes perfect sense."

There was a sudden silence. When Tao finally responded, there was an edge to his tone.

"I didn't consider myself single and available."

Monique let out a loud breath. This is what it should come down to. This is what hurt the most. Did she really have the right to be upset with him? She was the one who had insisted on casual and convenient, no romantic expectations. She was such an idiot!

"Look, we need to talk, Monique. In person. Let's just put everything on the table. Do you want to come by tomorrow after work?"

She closed her eyes while her lips started to tremble. Tears pooled behind her lids and slowly started to spill over. It took all of her willpower to answer him with a clear voice.

"Okay."

"Okay," he replied with obvious relief. "I'll be home by seven. Just come by any time after."

Monique nodded, unable to speak.

"See you tomorrow," Tao added before saying good-bye.

The next twenty hours were like torture. Monique decided to stay in the office late and go straight to Tao's apartment rather than go home first. She wrapped up her work at about six-fifteen, then spent more than twenty minutes in the bathroom trying to correct some damage caused by days of crying. Finally, she gave up and accepted that her eyes were going to be red and puffy and her lips would remain swollen and chapped. But at least she looked decent in her dark grey pencil skirt and crisp white blouse. She also made sure to wear her power pumps with the three-inch heels and pointed toes. Last, Monique had spent extra time that morning to wash and blow-dry her hair, then flat iron it to perfection. It still looked sleek and glossy.

She got down to Market Street just after seven o'clock and parked her car a couple of blocks west of Tao's building. She walked along the sidewalk with determined strides, her head held high, wearing sunglasses to cover her bruised eyes. As she passed the front of a restaurant, she took note of a small group of people who appeared to be waiting for a table. There was something familiar about one man in particular. He was wearing a sharp brown suit, but his back was to her, and Monique just kept walking.

"Moni?"

She stopped in her tracks, then spun around. There was only one person who ever called her that.

"Donald," she stated.

He walked toward her with a gente smile on his lips.

"Wow," he said, looking her up and down. "You look great."

He looked older, she thought to herself.

It was at least eight months since they had last seen each other, yet Monique did not remember the specks of grey in his hair, or the deep wrinkles in his forehead.

"Thanks," she replied politely. "What are you doing here? This is a little far from Oceanside."

"I'm about to have dinner," he explained with a head nod toward the crowded restaurant Monique had noticed earlier. "How are you doing?"

"I'm great!" she told him with a big smile and firm tone. Her oversized sunglasses hid the evidence of anything different.

Donald took a step closer to her, near enough to whisper.

"I'm glad. I know I have no right to say this, but I miss you."

Monique didn't know what to say. The truth was, at that moment, she didn't even recognize him as the man she thought she could not live without only a few months ago. Right now, she barely remembered anything beyond his name, and certainly did not miss anything about their disastrous relationship. She was about to say something dismissive when she noticed a woman step out of the entrance of the restaurant and look toward them. Monique didn't know her, but there was something about her eyes that seemed oddly familiar.

Donald noticed Monique's gaze and looked over his shoulder. He gave Monique a guilty, panic-stricken look, then walked quickly back to the woman.

"Who were you talking to, Donald?" she asked, her eyes still on Monique. "Who is that woman?"

Monique knew she should walk away, but something made her stay and watch as things unfolded.

"No one, Janet. Just someone I used to work with. Is our table ready?"

Maybe it was pure women's intuition, but Janet's eyes never left Monique's face and she wasn't about to be distracted.

"Don't lie to me, Donald. I saw the way you were talking to her. Who is she?"

The restaurant door opened again and two more women stepped out onto the street, one of whom was Tammy. Seeing the three women together said everything and suddenly, Monique knew exactly why Janet seemed familiar.

Chapter 22

The scene was like something out of a bad movie. Monique was there, experiencing the drama firsthand, but it felt as though it was happening to someone else and she was just a spectator.

Donald continued trying to distract his wife, but she kept questioning him, her voice getting increasingly loud and shrill. Tammy's youngest sister—Monique remembered her name was Emily—was trying to understand what was going on, asking questions, though no one would answer her. Tammy just looked at Monique for a long moment, then took a couple of steps toward her.

"Monique, how do you know my brother-in-law?"

Monique was frozen. She wanted so badly to lie or just run away. But, she could not stop looking at Janet Sutherland, confronted with a truth she finally couldn't ignore anymore.

"Donald and I worked together a while back," she told Tammy.

He must have heard her answer, because Donald seized the opportunity to get indignant.

"See? Are you satisfied, Janet? Look at the scene you've caused. Now you know why I don't take you anywhere!" he told her.

Monique could hear the scorn and insult in his voice. She whipped off her sunglasses and walk past Tammy, who was still looking at her with suspicion, and right up to Donald.

"Don't you dare talk to her like that!" she said slowly, her precise words dripping with disdain. "Tell her the truth. Tell her that you don't take her anywhere because you might run into one of your lovers. Tell her that you and I were together for three years, and you kept telling me over and over that you were practically separated, that your wife was a crazy bitch, and to give you more time. Tell her that you asked me to marry you, then coerced me into buying a house that you promised we would live in together. Tell her the truth!"

There was only shocked silence when Monique finished screaming into his face. Then Janet started sobbing.

"No, no, no. Oh, Donald! How could you?" she lamented.

"Oh my God," added Emily, looking back and forth between everyone there, clearly shocked and confused.

Donald was initially at a loss for words, totally unprepared to deal with Monique's raw honesty. His meanness disappeared quickly, replaced by oily, beseeching words that sounded childish and whiny.

"Come on, Janet. You can't believe what she says. She's lying! I barely know her! You know I love you . . ."

Monique turned away, disgusted by how familiar his speech was and not wanting to see Janet fall for the act. She took a step and came face to face with Tammy, whose eyes were burning with rage.

"You bitch!" she spat.

"Tammy, you don't know . . ." Monique started to explain in a weary voice.

"Shut up! You were sleeping with my brother-in-law? And the whole time, you were pretending to be my friend?"

"You think that I knew who he was? I didn't know!"

Tammy just shook her head and looked at Monique like she just crawled out from under a rock. Her distain pushed a button in Monique.

"Do you really think this is my fault, Tammy? Yes, I knew he was married, but you know as much as anyone that I believed what he told me. I thought their marriage was over. You were there when I finally understood that I had been used for three years. I cried on your shoulder in the bathroom at work! And you want to believe that I knew he was married to your sister? Are you crazy? Or maybe it's just your guilty conscience talking. You're the one who pretended to be my friend, then decided that you wanted the man I was with. Who's the bitch, Tammy?"

"Oh please! Tao doesn't belong to you. Even you said you guys aren't serious. You're just pissed off because men only want you for one thing. You give away sex, and they take it. You're not woman enough to keep them beyond that."

Tammy's ugly words made Monique want to slap her. But she clenched her fist instead, resisting the urge to do physical damage right there in front of a crowd of curious on-lookers.

"Good-bye, Tammy," she said in a quiet, cold voice, then walked away, refusing to look back at the drama still unfolding in front of the restaurant.

Though she headed in the direction of Tao's apartment, Monique was in no shape to see anyone, particularly him, at the moment. She walked past his condo and down a few more blocks before stopping at a Starbucks. After ordering a bottle of water, she headed into the bathroom and locked herself in a stall. Her face immediately crumpled and her body shook with every deep sob. After days of crying over Tao, Monique was surprised that there were any tears left in her eyes. Yet here she was again, out of control.

She sucked in a deep breath, trying to control her emotions. Monique wasn't crying over Donald. He was so insignificant to her now. It was everything else about that embarrassing scene that cut her deep. For the first time, Monique clearly saw the results of her participation in an extramarital affair. She watched a woman lose hold of her reality and have to face the truth about her husband.

Monique lost what she thought was a good

friendship. She had spent the last few days angry and disgusted with Tammy's behavior on Saturday night. But there had been a part of her that wanted to believe that Tammy had been drunk and unaware of her actions. Seeing the malicious intent on her face and hearing the callous justifications of her actions erased all of Monique's doubts.

Finally, Monique let out a deep breath, feeling as though the breakdown had passed. She used bathroom tissue to clean off her face before stepping out of the stall. Surprisingly, her face didn't look too bad in the mirror, and she left the bathroom soon after.

It only took her about ten minutes to walk back to Tao's place, but it was now almost eight-thirty. Hopefully, he would not ask her why she was so late. Monique was not prepared to divulge all the details of a disastrous evening so quickly.

She took a deep breath before knocking on his door. Tao opened it quickly. They said hello quietly, cautiously, and Monique followed him inside.

"I wasn't sure if you would be hungry, but I picked up some Chinese food for us," he told her.

"Thanks. Maybe I'll have some a little later."

He nodded and led her farther into the living room. She sat on the couch and he then sat beside her.

"I'm glad you came tonight, Monique. To be honest with you, I was starting to think you had changed your mind."

"Sorry," she told him. "I got delayed at the last minute."

"No worries. You're here now."

"So, where do we begin?" asked Monique.

There were many questions that she wanted to ask, but she was more interested in what he had to say at that point.

"Well, let's talk about us," he stated. "I think we can agree that our arrangement just isn't working. I mean, it's working in the sense that I enjoy being with you. You know . . ."

Monique just listened quietly, surprised to hear him stammer and stutter his words.

"I'm just saying that I think we have moved beyond the casual arrangement we had. I've moved beyond that," he clarified.

"I agree, Tao. I thought I knew what I wanted at the beginning, but I was wrong. I figured that if there were clear rules, no one would get hurt."

"Monique, you can't always protect yourself from getting hurt in a relationship. It's part of the territory."

"I know! It was stupid," she admitted. "So, what now?"

"We throw away your stupid rules, that's what," he stated, flashing her a teasing smile.

Monique could not help grinning back.

"What about your stupid rule?" she snapped back.

"Honesty? Sorry, that one stays."

"So that's it? We get rid of my rules? Then what?"

Tao shrugged before replying. "We continue

the way we were going. I was getting used to the romantic stuff actually," he stated, and she giggled, feeling better and lighter than she had in days. "I actually found it really hard not to wrap my arms around you in front of everyone on Saturday night."

Monique's smile faded a little. She really wanted to keep their positive discussion going, but she had questions. She needed to understand what happened on Saturday night, and it would be a mistake to ignore the issue. The memory of the look on Janet Sutherland's face was proof of that.

"So, what happened between you and Tammy?"

"Nothing," he replied immediately.

"So, you weren't the one who invited her to the party?"

"Yes, I did invite her, but only because I thought you were going to bring her anyway."

"Why didn't you tell me that you had seen her? More than once?" Monique insisted.

"I don't know, Monique. It didn't seem important. Her sister lives near here, and I just saw her in the neighborhood. That's it."

"Then, suddenly, she's kissing you in your bedroom. Come on, Tao. We just agreed to be honest. Are you saying there was no clue that she might be interested in you? No flirting? Nothing?"

"What do you want me to say, Monique?" he replied, getting defensive. "Yes, we talked a bit over breakfast once. I didn't ask her out or anything, I just ran into her and her sister at a restaurant. And she flirted a bit. But I didn't think anything of it."

Monique just looked at him, trying to believe his words, but suddenly feeling the pinch of insecurity.

"You talked," she repeated. "Over breakfast. It sounds a bit like a date."

"Oh, please! Look, I've told you what happened. I can't force you to believe me. I have nothing to hide. You and I were just casual at the time anyway."

His words hit her somewhere in the lower stomach. They echoed Tammy's accusations a little too closely. *Men only wanted you for one thing. You give away sex, and they take it.*

"That's right, we were just having sex. Was Tammy willing to give you something more?"

Tao looked at her hard, clearly frustrated with the direction of her questions, but trying to be patient.

"I don't know, Monique. What difference does it make?"

"It makes a big difference, Tao. Were you looking for a more committed relationship? Something I wasn't ready for?"

"Yes! Yes, I wanted more than what we had," he admitted. "The casual thing was your idea. I just went along with it because I liked you, Monique."

"Or you wanted what I was giving away for free?" she whispered in a hurt voice.

"What? I just told you that I wanted a committed relationship with you."

"No," Monique stated, cutting him off. "You

said you wanted a committed relationship, and there you were going out with Tammy and flirting with her at the same time. Then, you're kissing her. Apparently, a relationship with her would work just fine too."

"Monique, I don't even know what you're talking about. You're totally twisting my words."

"I heard everything you said, Tao," she stated as she stood up. "I can't do this."

The shock on his face would have been comical if Monique wasn't so upset. Suddenly, she could not get the sight of him kissing Tammy out of her mind. *Men only want you for what they can get. You give them sex, and they take it. You're not woman enough to keep them.* There was no way that she was going to put herself in the same situation again. She was never going to be the woman on the side again.

"Monique! This is crazy! Tammy has nothing to do with us."

She was already by the front door. Tao rushed to try and stop her from leaving.

"Tao, you were having sex with me, and starting something more serious with my friend at the same time. I'm sorry but I won't be used again. I have to go."

"Monique!"

He reached out to grab her arm, but she evaded his grasp and slipped out the door.

Chapter 23

New Year's Eve in San Diego was one big party. The streets were still lined with Christmas decorations, but every restaurant and bar was advertising a special bash to bring in the new year.

Tao left his apartment a few minutes before one o'clock that afternoon to head up to Gary's place. His plan was to hang out for a couple of hours before hopping on the highway for the drive up to Bakersfield. His mom had gone to Jamaica for Christmas, returning a couple of days ago. Tao would celebrate the night with her and a few family friends, then stay in town for the weekend.

When he got to Gary's house, he found his friend outside washing his car. They had not seen each other since Tao's housewarming party, and the men hugged briefly, exchanging belated Christmas wishes.

"Do you want a beer?" asked Gary as he took a gulp of his own dark brew.

"Nah, I'm good. Do you have any juice?"

"Sure."

Inside the house, Gary poured Tao a glass of fruit punch. They then went into the living room and Gary switched on the television and tuned it to a football game.

"You're heading up to Bakersfield right after this?" Gary asked.

"Yeah. It'll take me about four hours, and I want to get there before eight."

"It's too bad you're not staying here, though. Nicole is having a big party and hired Albert to DJ. That guy is annoying as hell, but damn, he can spin."

"Sounds like it will be hot," Tao commented. "But, I haven't visited my mom in a while. Work's gotten a little crazy here, so if I don't go now, I won't be able to go again for months. She's still pissed at me for not going with her to Jamaica."

Gary nodded. They sat in silence for a while, watching the game.

"How are things going with Melissa?" Tao asked.

Gary smiled like a satisfied cat.

"That good, huh?" laughed Tao.

"Yeah, it's pretty good. It's only been about two weeks, and I can't stop thinking about her. We talk every day, and laugh about everything. She's really cute, and just . . . normal."

Tao couldn't help chuckling again.

"I thought normal was boring for you?" he teased.

"Don't get me wrong. She's hot! There's nothing normal about what happens to me when I look at her. We haven't done anything yet, really, but man, I can hardly wait."

Tao just looked at Gary with a tolerant smile, but inside, he felt a bit of envy. That's how he had felt about Monique while they were together. There was no doubt in Tao's mind that he would still feel it if he ever saw her again. Feelings that deep and strong didn't just disappear in a few weeks.

"Is she going to Nicole's with you?"

"No, she and Monique are going to meet me there."

"That's right. She's a friend of Monique's," stated Tao softly.

"Her best friend's sister, actually."

Tao nodded, trying not to create an awkward moment. Gary knew that he and Monique were no longer seeing each other, but Tao had purposely been sketchy on the reasons. So far, Gary was respecting his privacy. The truth was, Tao didn't understand what went wrong, and still could not make sense of their final confrontation. But, Monique had been pretty clear about her wishes, so he had let it be and tried to put his attention into moving on. It wasn't going so well so far.

"Look, Tao, tell me to shut up if you want, but you've got to talk to her. You're miserable, she's miserable. It just doesn't make sense to me," Gary told him. "I asked her what happened, and she kind of said the same thing you did, that it just wasn't going to work. Anyone can see that there is something more going on."

Tao shrugged, then spent a few seconds examining the ice in his drink.

"I've gone over our last conversation a million times, Gary. I honestly don't know what happened. It started out fine. We both agreed that we wanted to have a real relationship, and forget that stupid idea of just being casual partners. Then she brought up Tammy, and all hell broke loose."

"Tammy?"

Tao nodded.

"I explained that she only kissed me because she was drunk, but Monique didn't believe me. She got it in her head that I was somehow seeing Tammy behind her back the whole time."

"Were you?" Gary asked, with serious, probing eyes.

"Come on, man! I told you, I ran into her, *once*, and she and her sister sat with me for breakfast. It was completely innocent. The only other time I saw Tammy was a couple of days before my party and I invited her only because I thought Monique was going to bring her anyway."

"I hear what you're saying, but you have to look at it from Monique's point of view. Particularly considering what she went through with that guy, Donald."

"The married guy, right?" asked Tao.

"Yeah. Did she tell you about him?"

"She mentioned him, briefly," said Tao.

"Well, she and I never really went into detail about it, but, basically, he strung her along for years, promising his marriage was over. I can see why she would run from any hint of cheating, Tao."

Tao looked into his glass again, wishing it held the answers.

"What's going on with you and Tammy now?" Gary finally asked.

Tao shrugged.

"Nothing really. We met for dinner once, and she stopped by last week before Christmas to say hi. I don't know. She's cool, we talk."

"I take it that she and Monique are no longer friends?" asked Gary in a dry tone.

"I guess not. Tammy hasn't mentioned Monique really. I told her we stopped seeing each other and that was the end of it."

"Well, it looks like she made a move on you knowing that you and Monique had something going on. That's pretty foul, man," stated Gary.

"I don't think it was like that. You saw how drunk she was that night? She could barely stand up. And Monique was the one who wanted to keep our relationship under wraps. Tammy was just doing some harmless flirting."

"Casual or not, there is a line you just don't cross with your friends, man," Gary insisted.

"I don't know. There's nothing going on between Tammy and me anyway. We're just friends. And Monique doesn't want anything to do with me, so what difference does it make?"

"Like I said, talk to her. Start over. Do something! You guys are making me depressed with all your moping."

Tao chuckled, but let the subject drop.

Gary wasn't suggesting anything he hadn't thought of himself. He had probably picked up the phone a dozen times to call Monique. But his pride wouldn't let him. He had gone along with her wishes from the beginning, taking whatever she was willing to give him despite his own wants, just to be with her. He had never lied to her. Yes, maybe he should have told her about running into Tammy, but their relationship was supposed to be casual. It was unfair of Monique to make demands on him after the fact. And yet she was keeping secrets of her own.

Why had they never talked more about this guy, Donald? Clearly, he had a big impact on her life. He was probably the reason she wanted only a casual relationship to begin with. Yet Monique never talked to Tao about it, other than that first night he drove her home. That stung.

Tao still remembered the feeling of powerless dread when she walked out of his apartment that last night. He could see the determination in her eyes. She had decided to end their relationship, and nothing he said was going to change her mind. She took his heart in her hand and carelessly tossed it away. Tao wasn't ready to forgive her for that. Nor was he interested in handing it to her again. She didn't need to know that he still woke up every morning thinking of her, wanting her so bad it was almost painful.

The men let the subject rest and moved on to talking about various other people they both knew. Tao stayed until just after three o'clock, then headed up to his mom's house.

* * *

It was almost ten-thirty that night when Monique arrived at Nicole's house for the New Year's Eve bash. Melissa also lived in Mission Valley, so Monique picked her up on the way.

The women ended up talking about Gary during the drive. Monique had followed Cara's advice and finally introduced them before Christmas. Other than to say that he thought she was nice, Gary had pretty tight lips with Monique about how things were going so far. Melissa, on the other hand, didn't seem to be able to shut up about what a great guy Gary was.

Monique just listened and smiled. She was really glad that two close people in her life may have found something special together. Of course, it was too early to tell, but they both clearly felt that elusive and intangible spark.

When they arrived at Nicole's house, there were so many cars on the block that Monique had to drive a few streets away to find parking. The women walked back to the house, meeting several other party-goers along the way. Gary was waiting for them near the front door. His face lit up when he saw them. Monique was pretty sure his delight was not directed at her.

The three of them went into the party and were quickly swallowed up in the crowd. The music was booming, and the drinks were flowing. There were people dancing everywhere they could find an empty spot. Gary took Melissa's hand and led her to a tiny opening near the back wall of the living room. They immediately started dancing to a big hit hip-hop song.

Monique watched them with an amused smile on her face, thinking they were really cute. She then made her way to the kitchen to get a much-needed drink.

The night progressed smoothly, with everyone enjoying the festive vibes and great music. The countdown to the new year was timed perfectly. Nicole and a few other people passed out party hats, noise-makers, and small glasses of champagne. Albert, as the DJ, turned down the volume and led the chant in seconds down to the stroke of midnight. The cheers of "Happy New Year" and well wishes were deafening as everyone hugged and kissed the people closest to them.

Monique had found Melissa and Gary in time to share the moment with them, but then wandered off to congratulate the other people she knew. She then spent the rest of the party near the kitchen, chatting with some of the other single women there.

By two o'clock in the morning, she was exhausted, physically and emotionally. Thankfully, Gary offered to drive Melissa home and Monique was able to head home by herself.

Though she had put on a happy face and forced herself to socialize, the night had been painful. It was very odd to her, because Monique had never been the kind of girl to hang out with her boyfriend. In college, she had been too busy to party, or seriously date anyone. And the relationship with Donald never allowed for nights out in public places while holding hands and smooching. So why was it so hard for her now to go anywhere social by herself? Why did the sight of another couple kissing or talking intimately make her want to cry?

When the hell are my tear ducts going to finally dry up?

Monique entered her dark house, kicked off her shoes, and walked straight to the bedroom without bothering to turn on the lights. She stripped off the very pretty party dress that she had bought for the night, tossing it on the floor without care. She climbed into the bed, not even bothering to remove her makeup or tie up her hair. Thankfully, sleep came quickly.

The next morning brought a decision and a determination that Monique had not felt in weeks. She was going to talk to Tao. The details weren't all clear yet. Finally, after a few weeks of hard thinking, she was absolutely certain that she wasn't ready to walk away from what they had and the relationship it could become.

It had only taken a few hours for Monique to regret her actions that last night with Tao. Even while they were having that stupid conversation, she knew that she was being irrational. Tao wasn't Donald and she wasn't Janet. She had just used the whole Tammy thing as an excuse because she was scared. Petrified to open up to love again and find out that what she had to give wasn't enough.

But it was too late. Somewhere between what should have been convenient sex and those weeks in the end when they connected, held hands, really talked about their thoughts, Monique had fallen in love with Tao Samuels.

Monique wasn't sure exactly what she was going to say to him, or how to explain why she had walked out that day. But the answer was in honesty. It was time for her to tell Tao about Donald and all the damage she now knew that relationship had caused in her life. She hoped he would understand and they could have a chance to move past it.

She would never know if she didn't try, and Monique could not live with not knowing.

Chapter 24

The normal thing to do was call Tao and ask him to meet. Monqiue thought about it, but just couldn't bring herself to dial his number. What if he sounded cold and detached? She would probably lose her nerve to say what she needed to. Or worse, what if he said he didn't want to see her? Her imagination created several other disappointing scenarios along those lines, so Monique decided the best solution was to go to his apartment. At least then she would have the opportunity to talk with him face to face.

Other than several phone calls to family in Detroit, and friends all over, Monique spent most of New Year's Day around the house, trying not the think about her plan. Part of her thought that maybe Tao would call her, take that step to fix things between them, but he didn't. Then she started to have second thoughts about the whole thing. Finally, she called Gary.

"Hey, Gary, Happy New Year," she stated when he answered.

"Monique? Happy New Year to you too! Did you get home okay last night?"

"Yeah, I was good. Did you and Melissa stay much longer?"

"Nah. The party started to wrap up at around three o'clock. We helped Nicole clean up a bit, then left. It was a great party, though."

"It was," she agreed, then took a deep breath before getting to the point. "Listen, Gary, do you have second?"

"Yeah, sure. What's up?"

"I don't know what Tao has told you about what's happened between us, but I think I made a mistake," Monique stated.

"What do you mean?" he asked.

"You know we broke up, right? It was my fault. I told Tao that I didn't want to see him anymore, but I made a big mistake. I freaked out over nothing and I need to try and fix things. I know this might be an awkward question, but do you think he's willing to talk about it?"

It felt like forever before Gary responded.

"Finally! One of you guys has come to your senses," he stated. "Have you called him? What did he say?"

"No, I haven't spoken to him since before Christmas," she explained. "He hasn't called me either. I was thinking of going to his place, maybe tomorrow?"

"No, you can't. Tao's not here. He went to Bakersfield to spend New Year's with his mom. I don't think he will be back until Sunday."

"Oh."

He must have heard the disappointment in her voice.

"Why don't you just call him on his cell phone?" suggested Gary.

"No, I need to do this in person, Gary. I don't think I will be able to explain things properly over the phone."

"Okay, then go see him on Sunday. I'll see if I can find out what time he'll be back."

"Thanks, Gary."

"Are you okay, Monique?" he asked.

"I'm all right. It's just time for me to deal with some things. I've put it off too long, that's all. I just hope that Tao is willing to listen to me."

"Don't worry, I'm sure it will work out. I've never seen too more miserable people in my life!"

Monique smiled, knowing that Gary was trying to make her feel better.

"We'll talk about it more on Sunday," he continued. "Melissa invited me to her sister's house for brunch. You'll be there, won't you?"

"Really? That's great! Things must be going really well between you two," she stated, smiled more.

Gary chuckled.

"So far, so good. We're still celebrating from last night."

It took Monique a few seconds to understand what he was hinting at.

"Oh . . . Oh! Is she there with you?"

"Yeah," he admitted with a sheepish laugh.

"Well then! I'll let you go back to . . . whatever you were doing."

He laughed harder.

"Seriously, though, Gary, thanks for listening."

"No problem, Monique. Anytime. But we'll talk more on Sunday."

"Okay."

They hung up, and Monique felt much better, not just about things with Tao but for Gary and Melissa.

Sunday brunch was beautiful. The weather in La Jolla was surprisingly warm, and Cara set up the meal on the patio. Monique arrived a few minutes after Gary and Melissa, and brought her usual contribution of fruit and coffee. She went around and said hello to everyone with hugs and kiss.

Her goddaughters were as sweet as ever and swarmed her with squeals and hugs. They then dragged her into a loud game of tag around the garden, though at twenty months old, Meghan didn't quite understand the rules but just ran around, occasionally falling on her bum in the haste.

Monique eventually joined Mel and Cara in the kitchen as they put the final touches on the meal, then helped them carry the food outside. The conversation around the table was relaxed while they all discussed the holidays. They were about halfway through eating before Monique picked up on the vibes between Cara and her husband, Kyle. The two women stayed outside drinking coffee for a few minutes alone after breakfast while the others cleaned up.

"So, what happened in Los Angeles?" Monique finally asked.

Cara smiled shyly. She had finally taken Monique's advice and gone with Kyle to LA for a few days between Christmas and New Year's Day. They had left the girls with his mother.

"It was great. We stayed in his hotel near the hospital. He worked during the day and we spent every evening together talking, or going for a walk. I don't think we've done that since we were dating."

"That's great, Cara. Did you talk about your concerns that he might be cheating?" asked Monique.

"I didn't have to. He took me to the hospital and introduced me to everyone. They all said the same thing, that he spent all his time there during the week so that he could drive back home as early as possible on Wednesdays. I might sound crazy, Monique, but I looked into his eyes, really looked, and I knew there was no one else."

"That doesn't sound crazy at all. There are just some things that are intuition. You have to trust it."

"I think I started to panic because there was something missing between us, and the idea of another woman was an easy explanation. The truth is that we had just been neglecting our relationship, and I have to take equal responsibility for that."

"It's hard, though," Monique told her. "You're trying to juggle the kids, his career, your job. It happens."

"Well, we have to put our relationship first. Everything else is secondary. We are so lucky, we can afford help, and we have Kyle's parents who will take the girls anytime."

"And me," added Monique. "Just tell me when you need a break, and we can have a sleepover at my house and I can take them to the beach."

"It's a deal," Cara accepted, laughing at the idea of Monique trying to handle the two hyperactive girls by herself. "So, what about you? You look like you've lost weight. Are you okay?"

Monique looked out at the breathtaking view of the ocean from Cara's backyard. She tried to smile at her friend reassuringly.

"I'm okay. It's time for me to move on one way or the other."

They had spoken before Christmas about the ugly confrontation with Donald, Tammy, and her sisters, and her break-up with Tao. Monique took a few minutes now to update Cara on the decision to try to see Tao that night and try to work things out. She talked a little about what she would say to him and how she planned to handle his reaction either way. Cara was supportive but cautious, not wanting to see Monique hurt even further.

Mel came outside a few minutes later, and the discussion switched to frank and completely inappropriate details of her first night with Gary. There was lots of whispering and giggling, but nothing could remove the sparkle from Melissa's eyes. When Gary came out to say it was time for them to leave and catch a movie, the three women could barely keep a straight face.

Monique decided to leave at that time as well. As

they parted ways in the driveway, Gary let her know he had spoken to Tao earlier that morning. He had left Bakersfield that morning and would be home about three-thirty in the afternoon, depending on the traffic.

At exactly five minutes to four o'clock, Monique was standing in front of Tao's door. It took her another five minutes of pacing and deep breathing before she finally knocked. There was no answer right away, so she knocked again. When the door finally opened, Tammy was standing on the other side.

Monique was speechless and could only look back and forth from Tammy's smug smirk to somewhere over her shoulder for any sign of Tao.

"Tao's in the shower," Tammy finally stated.

"What are you doing here?" asked Monique.

Tammy let out a sharp laugh, then folded her arms and stuck out her hip in a defensive pose.

"What are *you* doing here? Did you leave something behind?" she replied sarcastically.

Monique tried to stay calm, but her heart was racing and it felt like it was cracking in two.

"I want to talk to Tao," she insisted.

"Like I said, he's in the shower. I'll tell him you stopped by."

"Tammy, I don't know what you're doing here, and I don't really care. I'll wait for him to come out."

Monique took a step forward to walk inside the apartment, but Tammy straightened and barred her entrance with her body and a hand on the door.

"Don't you get it? He's moved on, okay? I told you, women like you are good for only one thing. Sex, that's it. Tao and I have much more than that. So, why don't you go and find another husband to cheat with and get lost!"

"Get out of my way, Tammy."

"Make me," she growled, her eyes filled with anger and determination.

"What's going on?" Tao stepped into the foyer, clearly confused and unprepared to find two women in his doorway looking like they were about to get physical. "Monique? What are you doing here?"

Tammy stepped back a bit, but still had her body blocking Monique from coming in.

"I was just asking her the same thing, Tao," she added in a scornful tone.

Monique ignored her, unable to take her eyes off Tao. His hair was still damp from the shower and he was dressed in casual ball shorts and a T-shirt. He looked just as good as she remembered.

"Sorry to just show up like this, but I was hoping we could talk," she told him while looking directly into his face.

His expression held only surprise and confusion. He opened his mouth to reply, but was cut off by Tammy.

"We're busy, right, Tao? So, I think it's time for you to leave."

Just like that, the door was slammed in Monique's face.

Chapter 25

"What are you doing?" demanded Tao

He looked at the closed door, then back at Tammy; the surprised fog in his brain was finally starting to fade since he saw Monique. He stepped forward, ready to reopen the door, but Tammy would not move out of the way.

"Let her go, Tao. It's not worth it."

"What?" he said, barely hearing her.

All he could see was the look in Monique's eyes as she told him she wanted to talk. He stepped forward again, but Tammy still didn't move. They were now almost touching.

"Move out of the way," he demanded, firmly but quietly.

"Tao, come on. You don't want to talk to her. She's just playing games with you. Let her go. And, we'll go get pizza like we planned."

"Tammy move. I'm not kidding."

She got really still, and the look in her eyes became hard and murderous.

"You still want her, don't you? You bastard!"

Tao looked down at the floor and let out a deep breath.

"Look, Tammy . . ."

"No, don't try to explain. I get it. You were just using me, weren't you?"

"Tammy, you and I are friends, that's it. I . . ."

"No, that's bull and you know it! You knew that I was into you, Tao, and you used me. You let me believe that we were moving toward something more. And the whole time, you were just waiting for that bitch to come back."

He opened his mouth and closed it again. Was there some truth to her words? Nothing had happened between him and Tammy, not even a kiss, but he knew she liked him. Did he use her?

"I don't know, Tammy. I'm sorry if I gave you the wrong impression."

"You're sorry?" she snarled with an ugly laugh. "Yes, you're sorry! You're going to walk away from a good, decent woman for *her*? Do you know what kind of woman she is? She's nothing but a cheating slut! And if that's what you want, then you'll get what you deserve!"

Tao wasn't really listening to her words. All he could think about was how quickly he could get her out of the way and open the door. Monique had to still be there. She wouldn't just walk away. He was starting to feel desperate.

"It's simple, Tammy. I want to be with Monique, okay? I didn't mean to hurt you, but I'm in love with her. So, just move out of the way."

The words came out a little more harshly than he had intended, but Tammy seemed to relax her stance and Tao managed to step around her and open the door. The hallway was empty. Monique was gone.

"Damn it!" he whispered with complete frustration.

He stepped back inside and started to slip on his ball shoes, focused on finding her before she got too far.

"Did she tell you that she slept with my brother-in-law?" whispered Tammy.

"What?"

"She knew he was married, but she had an affair with him for three years. She destroyed my sister's life, Tao."

He stopped trying to tie his laces and stood up, looking hard at Tammy. There were tears pooled in her eyes, and her lips were trembling. Tao finally started to see things clearly for the first time.

"Is this what it all about, Tammy? Is this your way of getting back at Monique?"

"No, no, you don't understand . . ."

"I get it now. I'm such an idiot! This was your game all along, right? Cause problems between me and Monique so that you could hurt her?"

"No, I didn't know. I just found out," Tammy insisted, clearly a little afraid of the anger in Tao's face.

"When did you find out? Today?"

She paused, trying to come up with an answer.

"I think it's time for you to go," he told her simply.

"Tao, don't you care about what she did? She's a slut . . ."

"Don't say another word, Tammy. You're the one who's been offering up your body just to destroy our relationship. Who's the slut?"

"No, Tao, I swear that's not what I was doing . . ."

"GET OUT!"

Tammy shut her mouth and looked down at the floor. It took her a few seconds but she finally walked through the door, still open from Tao's rush to find Monique.

He stood there for a couple of minutes as everything came into context. While some things were now so clear, Tao now had many more questions to be answered. But nothing was as important as finding out what Monique had come to talk to him about. The need to know now burned in his heart and made his hands shake with anticipation.

Tao finished tying up his shoes, then grabbed his keys, cell phone, and wallet. On the way down in the elevator, he anticipated that she had been gone for about ten minutes. If he was lucky, he would be able to reach her before she got to her car. Once on the street, he dialed her number. She did not answer her cell phone for three agonizing rings.

"Hello," she stated.

He could hear the emotion in her voice, and his thoat tightened in response.

"Where are you?" he whispered.

"Tao?"

"It's me. Where are you, Monique?"

She didn't respond for a couple of seconds.

"I'm on the boardwalk."

He immediately looked south toward the bay.

"At Seaport Village?"

"Yeah," she whispered.

"Okay. Don't move. I'll be there in five minutes."

Tao hung up and immediately started running full speed down Market Street. He saw her the second he reached the wooded walkway just off the beach. She was standing a few yards away, looking out toward the water. Tao came to a full stop and tried to control his breathing. He used his palm to wipe away the sweat now pouring down his face, then dried off his hands on his shirt. Monique turned to look at him while he was still bent over, gasping for air. She started walking toward him, and he did the same.

They both stopped short, a few steps apart. He was the first to speak, his breathing a little more under control.

"Hey," he said while his eyes ran over her face, taking in her swollen eyes and the trace of tears still on her cheeks.

Monique tried to smile, but her lips quivered. She looked away from him, and Tao's heart melted at the sight of her vulnerability. He immediately closed the distance between them and pulled her into his arms. A sob shook through her body and he tightened his hold. It took all of his strength to control the moisture that gathered in his own eyes.

"Monique, please don't cry."

She seemed to come undone at his words, and he could feel every shudder as it snaked through

her body in uncontrollable waves. Her cries came
out with raw emotion even as she tried to muffle
them. Tao tucked her face in the crook of his
neck and ran a soothing hand up and down her
back. His own lips trembled, and he squeezed his
eyes tight. The tears came anyway and dripped
onto the top her head.

"Please, Monique, don't cry, baby. It's okay,"
he chanted.

Finally, her body relaxed and Monique seemed
in control again. "Sorry," she mumbled, still
pressed close to him.

"Don't be sorry," Tao whispered. He wiped his
eyes and kissed the top of her head.

"I'm okay now," she assured him as she pulled
away.

But her eyes were fixed over his shoulder.
Tao took her face into his hands, and used his
thumb to wipe away the remainder of the tears.
She let out a long, shuddering breath, then
finally looked up at him.

"I'm the one who is sorry, Monique."

She searched his eyes, tying to understand
what he was really saying.

"You're the one that I want," he continued. "I will
take whatever you're willing to give. Okay? We'll be
whatever you want, for as long as you want."

"What about Tammy?" Monique whispered.

"She doesn't matter. She never mattered. It
was all about you from the beginning."

"But, she was there, with you today . . ."

"Monique, listen to me. I made a mistake. I
thought she was being a friend and it was easy

to be around her while I tried to get my head straight about us. But I was wrong. Nothing ever happened between us, I promise," Tao insisted.

His eyes were shiny and urgent, praying that she would believe him.

She looked down, and Tao swallowed with fear.

"She told me about you and her brother-in-law," he stated.

Monique froze and looked up at him again.

"What?"

"Shhh. It's okay. Now I understand everything. And I realize that she was using me to get back at you. I'm sorry I didn't see it."

She stepped away from him and walked to the edge of the boardwalk, leaning forward on the wooden railing.

"What exactly did she say?" she asked.

"It doesn't matter, Monique. I don't care what happened with that guy, okay? It's in the past."

"No, it does matter. That's what I came to tell you today."

His heart sank.

"What? What do you mean?"

"I've been doing a lot of thinking over the last few weeks. About you and me, and about my relationship with Donald. I finally realized that I hadn't moved on. I had allowed his betrayal to define who I was and what kind of relationships I was going to have in the future. Then I met you."

She looked back at him. Tao tried to read her face to see where her words were going to take them.

"I met you and I wanted you. But, I was too scared to have anything more than something casual. I just didn't want to get hurt again. I was stupid and wrong. And I wound up hurting both of us."

"What are you saying, Monique?"

"I'm saying that I'm ready. Finally, I'm ready to put it all behind me and move forward with you. I don't care about labels and definitions; I just want you, Tao. If you still want me."

Her last words were barely a whisper, but her eyes were filled with her commitment and emotion. He stepped up to her and pulled her into his arms again. It was a long moment before he could speak.

"I've wanted you from the start, Monique Evans. Even with your crazy rules."

They both laughed a little, but were still too raw with emotion to part. Finally, Tao lifted his head.

"Now, I don't know about you, but I'm starving."

Monique giggled. "I could eat," she whispered.

"Okay, good. But, I think I need another shower. That run down here almost killed me!"

Monique laughed harder. She stepped back and looked into his eyes. Tao seemed to read her mind. He bent his head and pressed his lips against hers. They stayed locked in their embrace for a long moment, completely forgetting where they were. Streams of people passed them in every direction, occasionally glancing enviously at the loving couple still kissing against the backdrop of the setting sun behind the dark blue ocean.

Want more Sophia Shaw?

Turn the page for a preview of
MOMENT OF TRUTH
and
A RARE GROOVE

Available now wherever books are sold!

Moment of Truth

Chapter 1

Adam Jackson checked his watch for the third time in an hour. It was still only a few minutes after eight PM. He tried to hide his boredom as he looked around at the forty or so people mingling at the dinner party. Finally, his eyes found the back of his friend, Yvonne Grant, who was the host of the party. She seemed to be having a great time as she laughed with the group she stood with.

Adam had known Yvonne since high school, and they had become very good friends over the years. She and her husband, Calvin, lived in a spacious bungalow in a suburb of Orlando, Florida, and this party was a long-overdue housewarming. Yvonne would not hear of Adam missing it, and insisted it was time he started to go out and meet people instead of working all the time.

So, there he was, leaning against the wall at the

back of the dining room with only a glass of Jamaican white rum on ice to keep him company. Adam shook his cup, causing the ice to tinkle. He took another drink just as Calvin approached him.

"Hey, Adam."

"Hey," Adam replied with a slight nod. "How are things going?"

"Good, so far," Calvin told him. "How about you? Do you want another drink?"

"No, I'm good."

"Well, why don't you come outside? We're about to set up a game of dominoes and we need another player."

Adam shrugged.

"Sure, why not?" he accepted, then downed the rest of his rum before setting the empty glass on the dinner table.

Both men walked from the dining room toward the back entrance of the house. They passed Yvonne on the way, and she gave them an approving smile. It was obviously she who had pushed Calvin into coaxing Adam out of his solitude.

The game table was set up on the covered patio just off the family room. Adam and Calvin joined two of Calvin's friends, who were already seated. After quick introductions, the domino game got under way. The next couple of hours sped by, and several more men gathered outside to watch and occasionally play after each round.

By ten-thirty, the group was loudly laughing and slamming down domino bones with every play. Adam had just lost a match and was being subbed out. He gave up his chair and smiled at the ribbing from the other players, but was enjoying himself more than he had in a long time.

It was easily over two years since Adam had spent an evening hanging out with a group of guys. He was often invited out, particularly by Yvonne or his other friend, Vince, but always found some excuse, usually work. Now, he wondered why he had resisted.

As the next game got started, Adam stepped back into the house to use the bathroom. Yvonne walked over to him as soon as she saw him.

"Having fun?" she asked.

"I'm doing all right," he responded with a hint of a smile.

Yvonne's eyes immediately brightened, and she took his hand and gave it a quick squeeze.

"Do you want something to eat? I just put out some dessert."

"No thanks, I'm just going to run to the bathroom," he replied.

"Okay," she said, and squeezed his hand again before letting go.

The doorbell rang just as Adam turned into the powder room near the front of the house.

Cadence Carter let out a deep, calming breath as she waited outside her neighbors' door. She had just moved into the house across the street three weeks before, and had met Yvonne and Calvin earlier that week. They seemed like a nice couple, so Cadence had felt obligated to accept the invitation to their party. She really wasn't in the mood to socialize with strangers, but was committed to at least making an appearance.

Her plan was to make an appropriate excuse to leave after about an hour.

The front door opened while Cadence was shifting her grip on a bottle of South African merlot. The sounds of classic R&B music and conversation spilled out into the warm Florida night.

"You made it," Yvonne said with a warm smile. She was a tall, slender woman with a red-brown complexion.

"Hi, Yvonne, sorry I'm late," Cadence replied as she stepped inside.

"No worries, no worries."

"This is for you," Cadence added, handing Yvonne the bottle of red wine.

"How sweet, thank you. Come, let's get you something to drink."

Cadence followed Yvonne through the house and smiled politely as she passed groups of people chatting together, or swaying to the music. A bar was set up on a table near the kitchen, and Yvonne added Cadence's bottle to the other wine there.

"What would you like?" asked Yvonne.

"A beer is fine."

"Okay, I'll grab one out of the fridge."

While she waited for Yvonne, Cadence looked around at the house, which was quite similar to hers. The layout was pretty much the same. All the houses in the immediate area were built around ten years ago. A few were two-stories, but most were bungalows, like Yvonne's and the one Cadence had recently bought.

The party was clearly in full swing, with well over sixty people mingling around the house, while eating from small dessert plates or sipping a variety of drinks. There were about another twenty people out on the enclosed patio, mostly men. She recognized Yvonne's husband, Calvin, as he stepped through the sliding doors from outside. He nodded when he saw her and she waved back. Calvin started walking toward her, but was interrupted when approached by another guy. Cadence was immediately struck by how different the two men were as they stood side by side.

While Calvin was fairly average looking, with an open face and stocky build, his friend was anything but. It wasn't something obvious like his size or clothing, though he was tall, probably just over six feet, on the slender side, and dressed in a conservative shirt and slacks. What struck Cadence was the character and details of his features.

The first thing she noticed was his lips. They were full and well sculpted, with a boyish tilt at the ends. He wore a moustache, but it was thin, well groomed, and made him seem older. The next thing she noticed was how serious he seemed. His shoulders were rigid, and his jaw was set in hard lines. Even the way he spoke to Calvin suggested restrained impatience and restlessness. Cadence was sure it had been a long time since he had truly laughed.

She turned away from the men when Yvonne returned.

"Here you go," Yvonne said as she handed Cadence a chilled bottle of Corona with the cap removed. "Do you want a glass?"

"No, this is okay, thanks."

"So, are you finished unpacking?"

"Almost," Cadence replied after taking a small sip of beer. "Thank God I don't own a lot of things; otherwise it would take me forever to get everything in the right place."

"I know. We've been here for almost a year, and I still have unopened boxes in the garage." There was a small pause before Yvonne continued. "Is it just you?"

Cadence knew exactly what Yvonne was asking. It was the same question she got from the real-estate agent, lawyer, and mortgage specialist she had dealt with during her house-hunt five months ago. It seemed unbelievable to everyone that she was able to buy a home on her own at twenty-eight years old.

Her appearance probably didn't help, either. With her mass of thin dreadlocks hanging below her shoulders, and her penchant for jeans and flip-flops, Cadence knew that it was hard for business people to take her seriously. At five-foot, one inch, and 110 pounds, she also didn't look much older than eighteen.

"Yup, just me," Cadence responded simply.

Yvonne only nodded in a slow up-and-down motion. The additional questions were in her eyes but stayed discreetly behind her lips.

The tension was broken when Calvin approached them, followed closely by the guy he had been speaking to.

"Hi, Cadence. I'm glad you could come," Calvin said to her with a warm smile and his hand extended.

Cadence shifted her beer bottle to her left hand so she could shake his hand.

"Thanks again for the invite," she responded. Her own smile revealed the shallow dimples in her cheeks.

"Adam," Calvin said as he turned to the other man now standing between him and Yvonne, enclosing the four of them in a circle. "Cadence has just moved into the house across the street. Cadence, this is a good friend of ours, Adam Jackson."

"Hi," the two strangers said to each other.

There were a couple of minutes of polite chitchat about how nice the party was, and how many of the neighbors had attended. Then, Adam and Yvonne stepped away into the kitchen leaving Calvin and Cadence alone.

"So, how are the renovations coming?" Calvin asked Cadence.

"What a nightmare! My kitchen is a total mess," she replied. "I still can't believe that the contractor just disappeared."

Cadence had met Calvin the previous Tuesday when he spotted her struggling to bring in bags of supplies from her car. He had just parked in his garage, but jogged across the street when one of the bags broke, spilling its contents all over the driveway. After introductions, Calvin helped Cadence carry everything from the trunk of her car into her garage. One of those items was a new kitchen faucet.

Cadence met Yvonne the next day when she

saw the couple outside and went over to thank Calvin again.

"Did you find anyone to finish the job?" he asked.

She shook her head. "No. One of my sister's friends was supposed to come by today, but of course he didn't show up. I'm going to have to find someone else this week."

"Maybe Adam can help. He's in construction," he suggested. "Adam?"

Adam raised his head when he heard his name, then came back over to them.

"Hey, maybe you can help Cadence out," Calvin started. "Her kitchen was being renovated, but the contractor took off."

"Okay," Adam replied, but his tone indicated he was still confused.

"What exactly do you still need done?" Calvin asked Cadence when she and Adam stood in silence.

"Um, it's not a lot. The sink and faucet need to be put in, and some caulking still needs to be done."

"That doesn't sound too bad. Do you have everything you needed?" Adam asked.

He looked Cadence directly in the eyes for the first time, and she was momentarily frozen by the intensity reflected in them. She was also surprised at their color; a dark copper brown, several shades lighter than the cool chocolate of his skin.

"Yes," she stammered. "I think so."

Adam nodded, then glanced at Calvin, who only smiled back.

"Okay, I can probably stop by this week to have a look at it."

"That would be great! Thanks!" Her deep smile flashed the twin dimples. "I'll give you my phone number and you can call when you're available."

"There is a pen and a note pad in the kitchen," Calvin offered.

"I'll be right back," Cadence told them.

"What was that about?" Adam asked Calvin as soon as she was out of earshot.

"What?"

"Did Yvonne put you up to this?"

"Hey man, it's not that complicated. She needs some help, that's all."

Adam clearly didn't believe him, but held his tongue.

"Here it is," Cadence said when she returned and handed Adam the piece of paper. "I really appreciate your help."

"No trouble," Adam responded softly, then turned to Calvin. "I have to get going."

"So soon?" Yvonne asked as she approached him from behind.

"Yeah."

"Okay, I'll walk you out," offered Yvonne.

"Calvin, I'll speak to you soon," Adam stated as the men shook hands.

"You too, man. It was good to see you."

With a polite nod to Cadence, Adam left.

A Rare Groove

Chapter 1

"You're listening to GROOVE FM 99.1," announced the silky, sultry voice over the radio. "Atlanta's home for classic soul. This is Moni S taking you on a musical joyride. It's 2:50 p.m. on your midday, and we've just ended fifteen minutes of music with Georgia's own Jean Carn singing 'Don't Let It Go to Your Head' from her second album, *Happy to Be With You*.

"Folks, I will be away next week, but Sweet Marie will be here to take care of you. It's Friday, so have a beautiful weekend. Right now I'm going to leave you with Eugene Record, 'Trying to Get to You,' on GROOVE FM 99.1."

The music faded in just as Simone turned off the microphone and swung her chair away from the computer screen.

"Good show, Moni," said her producer, Michael

Thompson. "We got about thirty text messages during that last rare groove hour, not to mention a whole slew of e-mail."

Simone smiled. Her show, called the *Midday Joyride*, ran from 10:00 a.m. to 3:00 p.m. Monday to Friday. A large number of her audience listened in while at work, and were always letting her know how they felt about the music she played. GROOVE FM was very different from the other radio stations in Atlanta. It was a small family-run business with a very specific market: rhythm and blues, soul, and funk from the 1970s, 1980s, and early 1990s. It was the type of music that everyone loved.

Michael and Simone both started to clean up the studio and file away the session's reports. Don Appleby, the on-air host for the afternoon rush hour, took over the microphone and prepared to start his show after the commercial and news break.

"Are you all set for your vacation?" Michael asked Simone once they had left the studio and started walking out of the building.

"Just about," she replied.

"I can't believe you're going to Jamaica," he stated with a big grin on his face.

"I know," she agreed. "I can't wait to relax on the beach."

"What time is your flight on Sunday?"

"About eight thirty in the morning," Simone replied with a grimace. "It will put me in Jamaica before ten thirty. Amy's wedding isn't until Friday, but we're having a four-day bachelorette party."

Up until about one year ago, Amy Tomkin was the receptionist at GROOVE FM. She was a bubbly, friendly girl, so when she left the station, she remained close with many former coworkers, Simone in particular. Her fiancé's mother was Jamaican, so when they decided on a wedding in Jamaica, she asked Simone to be her maid of honor. Simone accepted with pleasure.

"That's pretty early," Michael commented in reference to her flight.

"I know! I'm going to have to be at the airport before seven o'clock! I'm not looking forward to it. I am definitely not a morning person."

Michael laughed as he nodded with full agreement. Even though they both were in the office around nine o'clock in the morning, Simone could not crack a smile until at least eleven o'clock. She was a true professional, so the audience definitely could not tell the difference. But everyone in the studio knew to ignore her grumpy, sarcastic comments until her energy kicked in.

"How is Amy doing?" Michael asked.

"She's doing well. I thought she would be stressed out planning everything, but she said it was so easy. The hotel took care of everything."

"She and Cedric have been dating for as long as I've known her," he commented.

"I know. Almost ten years, she told me. They met in high school as freshmen. Isn't that romantic?" Simone said.

Michael just shook his head and twisted his lips, indicating he thought it was pretty sad. Simone continued, ignoring his cynical male perspective.

"And now they are getting married in paradise."

He couldn't help but smirk again. Simone was probably the most stunning woman he knew. Not only was she pretty, but she had this natural sex appeal that very few men could ignore. It wasn't just the sophisticated feminine clothes, or her perfectly manicured appearance; it was in her eyes, her smile, and even the way she walked. But anyone who knew Simone well knew that she was genuinely unaware of her sexual allure or the power it could have if used. She was a hopeless romantic that still believed in marriage and everlasting love.

A few minutes later, they were ready to part ways in the parking lot.

"Give Amy and Cedric my best."

"I will," Simone agreed before the two hugged. "See you in a week and a half."

"And don't go falling for an island man!"

She laughed out loud at his stern advice and was still smiling as they waved to each other from their cars on their way out of the parking lot.

The radio station was in the core of downtown Atlanta, so Simone headed toward the I-85, then north to Buckhead where she lived. Her apartment was in the heart of the booming suburb, near high-end shopping, trendy restaurants, and a vibrant nightlife. She was probably paying more than she should for a one-bedroom rental, but it was perfect for her needs right now.

When she got home, Simone turned on the stereo and headed into the bathroom. *The Best of Sade* played loudly while she filled the deep soaker tub with hot water and dropped in a moisturizing bath bomb. She then lit a series of lavender candles before removing her clothes and stepping into the water. The foamy bubbles covered her up to her neck.

Taking a long soak was Simone's favorite way to unwind after a show. However, on this afternoon, she would have to cut it short. She had a couple of appointments and several errands to do on Saturday, so her cleaning, laundry, and packing needed to be finished tonight. It had been at least a couple of years since she had gone away for more than a weekend, so Simone had no clue what she would need for a week in Jamaica that included a wedding and a prenuptial dinner.

She was also expecting a call from Kevin Johnson, the guy she was dating, later in the evening. He had left that morning for a business trip in Las Vegas, so they would not see each other again until she returned from her trip. She wasn't sure if he would still call since their last talk had resulted in a heated argument the night before.

Kevin was a retired professional boxer, and now owned a successful car dealership in the Atlanta area. He was born and raised in Atlanta, and was a real live version of the rags-to-riches story. The public and media loved him, so he was often asked to attend or speak at social events. He had invited her to a charity dinner Thursday evening, but Simone had decided not to go at the last minute. As someone in the media herself, she understood his life, but it still made her uncomfortable to stand beside him in the spot-light. She liked being in the radio industry because she could maintain a certain amount of anonymity and privacy.

She and Kevin had been dating for only about eight weeks, seeing each other about once a week. The event on Thursday would have been the second large social event they would attend together. The first was on their second date, and Simone had felt as if she were under the microscope all night long. It was not an experience she wanted to repeat so soon.

Kevin was not pleased when she canceled at the last minute, and could not understand her aversion to hanging on his arm at an expensive, high-society affair. Even after Simone had apologized for the third or fourth time, but made it clear that she was not going with him to the dinner, Kevin had called her a few names and hung up the phone. They had not spoken since.

Simone eventually stepped out of the bathtub and wrapped herself in a plush white robe. She threw on comfortable cotton clothes and got busy with her list of chores. By ten thirty, she was finished packing, except for a few toiletries and clothes she intended to buy on Saturday.

She had left a message on Kevin's cell phone during her dinner break a couple of hours earlier, but he still had not called back. She was tempted to call him again, but resisted the urge. Her pride said that if he wanted to stay angry with her, she was not going to chase him down. Simone went to bed shortly after.

Saturday started early with a hair appointment at nine o'clock for a relaxer touch-up and cut. Simone had planned to be out of the salon by noon, but her stylist, Tony, had triple-booked himself with a last-minute wedding party. Tony was extremely apologetic and promised to have her done in record time. Though he used an assistant to speed things up, Simone still did not leave the salon until almost two o'clock. As irritated as she was by the delay, Simone had to admit that her hair looked fierce. Tony had outdone himself with the style, giving her a short, sculpted cut with an angled fringe at the front and tapered low along her nape. It lengthened her square face and showed off her high cheekbones and cat-shaped eyes. He also took the time to show her how to style it in the Caribbean heat so it would be low maintenance on her trip. She could not have been happier with the results.

But the delay still ruined her schedule for the day. In the end, after running around for the next several hours, Simone did not get home until almost eight thirty that night. She finished her packing and final preparations, then crawled into bed, exhausted, just before midnight. She was up again at a quarter to five the next morning feeling as if her head were stuffed with cotton. The day then went from bad to worse.

Her cab was over twenty minutes late, so Simone ended up in an extremely long line at the airline check-in counter. Then, after shuffling along for almost forty-five minutes, she stood in front of the reservation representative, but suddenly could not find her passport. She spent the next couple of minutes in a mad panic, riffling through her over-sized purse as pens, gum, and miniature toiletries tumbled on the floor around her. Finally, she found it between the pages of a paperback novel, then had to pick up all her spilled items while the woman in line behind her tapped stiletto heels in annoyance.

Eventually, Simone made it to the boarding gate and even had a few minutes to grab a large coffee and a bagel. Her cell phone rang just as they were getting ready to board the plane. Simone debated whether or not to answer the call, then got concerned it might be urgent. She almost spilled the coffee trying to grab the call before it went to voice mail. It was Amy.

"Hey, Simone, I'm glad I got you," Amy said in a relieved voice. "I thought you may be on your flight already."

"We're just about to board. Is everything okay?"

"No," Amy replied after a long sigh. "We're not going to be flying out today."

"Why? What's wrong?" Simone asked urgently.

"Cedric has food poisoning or something. He's been throwing up since the middle of the night, and now he can't leave the bathroom. I think we're going to have to go to the hospital."

"Oh no! What did he eat?"

"I don't know! He was out with his work friends for most of the evening. Anyway, our flight leaves in a few hours, but I'm trying to reach our travel agent."

"Oh, Amy!"

Simone was about to ask more questions, but she heard the final boarding call announced for her flight.

"Amy, I have to go. I'll call you once I land, okay?"

"Okay."

"I'm sure it's nothing serious," Simone added. "Tell Cedric that I hope he feels better soon."

"Okay," Amy answered. "Have a safe flight."

Simone hung up and rushed to the gate before they closed it off. Once she was seated, it took her a while to get comfortable and settled. Her thoughts were mixed with concern for Cedric, sympathy for Amy, and wondering what she was going to do by herself on a Caribbean resort until they arrived.

Soon after takeoff, Simone was served breakfast and a glass of champagne. Eventually, she relaxed and even managed to sleep for over an hour. She woke up when their pilot announced the descent to Sangster International Airport in Montego Bay, Jamaica. He added that the temperature at ten o'clock in the morning was a sunny seventy-seven degrees Fahrenheit. Simone lifted the window screen and got her first view of the island as they approached from the west off the Caribbean Sea. Frothy blue water met creamy beaches and lush green vegetation covering rolling hills.

She smiled at the sight and started feeling more excited than she had in weeks.

Three hours later, Simone walked into the third-floor hotel room she was supposed to share with Amy until after the wedding on Friday afternoon.

She had spent the last hour since she arrived on the resort property having refreshments and listening to a presentation about the facilities while the room was being prepared. She also tried to reach Amy, but could not get an answer at the home number or on her cell phone.

Their room was a spacious suite with two queen beds and a separate sitting area that had a sofa, desk, and television. There was also a small balcony that faced the garden.

Simone's luggage had been brought up while she checked in, and was lying neatly on a bench next to the closet. She dropped her purse on her suitcase, then kicked off her shoes before falling back onto the bed closest to the window, claiming it as her own. Part of her wanted to curl up under the covers and take a nap; the other part wanted to change into shorts and flip-flops and walk around the grounds. She debated the options for so long that she eventually fell asleep.

She did not notice the voice mail message on her cell phone until midafternoon. After the nap, she took a shower and was unpacking some of her clothes into the closet when she heard the phone beeping. The display indicated a missed call from Amy. Simone used the room phone to listen to her message.

"Hey, Simone, it's Amy. Cedric and I are back at home. He did have a mild case of food poisoning, but the doctors said he should be fine in a couple of days. I'll call you later and let you know when I've rescheduled our flights. Sorry to leave you stranded, but we'll get there as soon as we can. Speak to you soon. Bye."

Simone looked around the room wondering what to do.

After she finished getting settled, she stepped out onto their small balcony and into the warm, breezy Caribbean air. The June weather in Atlanta was about the same temperature, but somehow the warmth of the sun felt different here. She leaned her hip against the rail and looked around at the vibrant garden spread before her.

Simone was about to turn away from the view and head back into the air-conditioned room when a flash of color caught her eye.

That was the moment she saw him for the first time.

Chapter 2

Simone was surprised to see a small swimming pool to the right of her room, secluded behind a row of low bushes and towering palm trees. He emerged from the water as he finished his swim. His back was to her and he slowly walked through the water toward the pool edge. Each step he took caused sunlight to reflect off his dark wet skin. His shoulders were thick and broad, then bunched with power as he used his arms to push his body out of the pool and swing his legs onto the patio around it. The water ran down his back in tiny rivers, then soaked into the red material of his swim shorts. The trunks rode low on his slender hips and clung to the tight round curve of his butt. She caught a glimpse of powerful thighs and calves before they were hidden behind the plants and foliage.

From what she could see, this man was the physical embodiment of masculinity. He had to be over six feet, and was all smooth skin and lean muscles. The way he moved suggested easy confidence.

The stranger reached for a towel that lay on a nearby lounge chair, and leisurely rubbed the short black hair on his head. Simone continued to watch his every move as he wiped off his shoulders and each arm before wrapping the towel low around his hips and securing it in place by tucking in one of the edges. She even leaned a little closer, anticipating the moment he would turn around. Her silver earrings flashed in the daylight and must have caught his eye. He turned around quickly and looked straight up at her, one hand shielding his eyes from the bright sun.

Simone froze, unsure of how to react. Should she turn away and pretend she didn't see him, or wave at him and hope he waved back? They looked at each other so long that it was too late to do anything. She felt her face go warm with embarrassment, but she still could not look away. To her surprise and delight, Mr. Tall and Dark dropped his arm and spread his generous lips into a wide smile, revealing perfect white teeth.

She flashed a quick smile of her own, then hurried off the balcony with her heart racing. Once in the hotel suite, she burst out laughing, charged with energy from the encounter. A few minutes later, she stepped out onto the balcony again, but the pool area was empty and her beautiful mystery man was gone.

It was only a few minutes after three o'clock. Simone decided to go for a swim, and the secluded pool downstairs seemed like the perfect spot. She quickly changed into her new two-piece white bathing suit and added a matching white tunic over it. She coated her exposed skin with sunblock, then threw her sunglasses, towel, novel, and room pass into a beach bag and headed downstairs.

It took a little bit of investigating before she found the right path in the garden that led to the secluded pool. It was still empty when she finally found it. She dropped her bag on the tiles, then tried to pull one of the three lawn chairs a little closer to the pool edge with one hand. It was made from a thick iron and much heavier that she expected. Her first tug only moved it about an inch. She leaned forward and pulled again harder with both hands. The sunblock lotion had left her fingers a little greasy and caused her grip to slip. Simone stumbled backward, then tripped over her bag. She went tumbling into the water with her arms and legs flailing.

Simone was not a very good swimmer and panic set in immediately. It took her a few seconds to realize that someone was in the pool with her and was trying to help her. Solid arms wrapped around her chest and quickly lifted her up and out of the water. She coughed roughly and tried desperately to gulp in air.

When her heart rate had decreased and she had calmed down, Simone found herself lying on the same lounge chair that had caused the mishap to begin with. She closed her eyes and took a few more deep breaths.

"Are you okay?"

The deep voice caught her off guard. Simone turned quickly to her right and looked into eyes so black they shone. His long, angular face was marked with lines of concern. She blinked repeatedly, trying to find her voice. Then that familiar brilliant smile appeared on his face.

"Oh!" she uttered, immediately realizing it was the stranger from earlier.

"Are you okay?" he asked again.

The smile was still in place and he now seemed more amused than worried. His voice was as smooth and velvety as his skin.

Simone cleared her throat. Water gathered in her eyebrows from her soaking hair and dripped down her nose. She wiped it away with the palm of her hand.

"I . . . I think so," she managed to croak out after a few seconds. She turned her face away and tried to stifle another rough cough. When she looked back at him, the smile had faded and the look of concern was back.

"I don't know how to thank you," she whispered.

"Don't worry about it. I was just walking by when I heard you scream."

Simone then noticed that he was wearing a light blue T-shirt and khaki shorts instead of his red swim trunks. The clothes were dripping wet and plastered to his body.

"Are you sure you're okay?" His question forced her eyes away from his chest and back to his face. "Let me help you back to your room."

"Oh," she uttered as he gently took hold of her arm and helped her up. "I'm okay, really."

He ignored her protest, picked up her bag, and urged her forward with one arm across her back. Simone gave in to his maneuvering and followed him toward her wing of the hotel. He didn't ask for directions until they were inside the building, and it then dawned on her that he recognized her from earlier. Her embarrassment doubled.

"My name is Maxwell, by the way. Maxwell Harper."

He had just let her go so that she could open her room door. The amused smile was back on his face.

"Nice to meet you, Maxwell Harper." She couldn't help but respond with a smile of her own. "I'm Simone St. Claire."

Maxwell nodded once.

When the door unlocked, Simone pushed it open and stepped over the threshold. She turned to face him while still in the doorway.

"Thank you, again. Thank God you were walking by when you did. And I'm sorry I got you all wet."

"No worries," he replied with a shoulder shrug.

"Okay, well . . . I guess I'll see you around the resort."

"How about for dinner?"

Simone just looked at him, not sure she had heard him correctly.

"I'm sorry," he quickly added and took a step back from the door. "You're here with your boyfriend or husband, right?"

She shook her head. "No. No, I'm not. I was supposed to meet my girlfriend, but she can't get here for another couple of days."

"Oh, okay." The smile was back. "So, would you like to meet for dinner?"

"All right," Simone replied before she could consider the wisdom of her decision.

"All right," he echoed. "How about I pick you up here at six o'clock?"

"Six o'clock it is."

Maxwell nodded again, then handed her the beach bag before he left.

Her conscience acted up while she was showering again to wash away the chlorine from the pool. She should not be going out with another man while she was technically dating someone else. Especially a man that made her feel warm in her stomach just by looking at him. But then she reasoned that she was on holiday, and it was a harmless dinner with another vacationer. Plus, it was now three days since she had heard from Kevin, and at this rate, their first fight might be their last.

Maxwell returned as scheduled, and Simone met him in the hall. After a brief greeting, they made their way toward the dining area of the resort in silence. Simone spent most of that time checking him out with her peripheral vision. As she had suspected, he had to be at least six feet three inches tall. She was a tall girl at five feet nine in her bare feet. Tonight, she was wearing sandals with a low heel, yet the top of her head just cleared his collarbone.

"How are you feeling?" he asked once they had been walking outside for a couple of minutes.

"I'm fine. My throat is a little sore, but that's it."

"Good."

"I just can't believe that I fell into the pool like that."

"You fell in? I thought you were trying to swim."

"No! I'm not the best swimmer but I'm not that bad," she told him. "I was just trying to move the chair closer to the pool, but my hand slipped. The next thing I know, I'm falling backward into the water."

Simone was laughing by the end of the story. He was laughing too, and it came out in a low, melodic hum.

Maxwell directed her toward one of the several restaurants that overlooked the ocean. He opened the door for her, then escorted her in with a light hand on her lower back.

"I think we might need reservations here, Maxwell," she told him while they waited to be greeted. "At least, I think that's what they said at the orientation this morning."

The hostess arrived before he could respond. Maxwell gave his last name, and they were quickly seated in front of a window with a view of the beach.

"I had made reservations for myself yesterday when I arrived," he told her.

Simone nodded. Their waiter arrived and took their drink and meal orders.

"So, Maxwell Harper, what brings you to Jamaica?" she asked.

"Family," he said simply.

"Really? Like a reunion?"

"Sort of."

She nodded, a little perplexed by his short, cryptic answers.

"Are you all staying at the resort?" she asked, trying to understand him but not be too nosey.

"No, I think I'm the only one right now. Most of them are staying with my aunts and uncles in Mo Bay."

"So you're Jamaican? You sound American," stated Simone, unable to mask her surprise.

Maxwell smiled easily, dispelling her feeling that he was being evasive. "Both actually. Born in Jamaica, raised mostly in Atlanta."

"No way!" exclaimed Simone. "I'm from Atlanta. Which part?"

"College Park."

"I grew up around Druid Hills, but I live in Buckhead now. That is such a coincidence. Who would have thought I would come all the way to the Caribbean and the first person I meet is from the ATL!"